TANDEM

A Fistful of Dynamite

Juan Mirandez Ibanez never met a man he
wouldn't kill . . . until the day he met John
Mallory. There was something about the
Irishman's style that fascinated Juan. Maybe it
was the way Mallory ignored Juan's gun and
coolly asked for a light.

Then John Mallory opened his jacket and Juan
knew for sure why he wouldn't kill him. Strapped
to Mallory were sticks of dynamite, detonators
and fuses – enough to take Mexico, and Juan
Mirandez Ibanez, off the map for ever!

Suddenly, Mallory took the cigarette Juan had
lit and flung it towards the stage coach.
'Duck, you sucker,' said the Irishman calmly –
just before the explosion . . .

A Fistful of Dynamite

James Lewis

TANDEM
14 Gloucester Road, London SW7

Originally published in the United States by Universal
Publishing & Distributing Corporation, 1971 as *Duck, You
Sucker!*
Published in Great Britain by Universal-Tandem
Publishing Co. Ltd, 1972

Made and printed in Great Britain by
Hunt Barnard Printing Ltd., Aylesbury, Bucks.

PART ONE

JUAN

PART ONE

Chapter One

Mexico, 1913

He had been there for more than an hour. Overhead, a
blood red sun burned its way slowly toward the mountains, and the scorched dusty plain spread out endlessly
around him. Squatting on the dry ground, he could feel
the heat singe his feet through his boots.

Juan Miranda Ibanez raised his sombrero and squinted
into the shimmering distance. Nothing. Only low scrub
and an occasional nopal cactus. He pushed the soft hat
down over his eyes. It could not be much longer now.

A sudden ache in his bladder made him rise and amble
toward the only tree in sight. Half of Mexico to pee in, he
laughed, and like a dog I head for a tree. He pushed aside
a dirty shirttail and unbuttoned his pants. To the side a
line of flying ants marched stolidly across the dry terrain.
He turned slightly and aimed at them.

There was a low dust cloud on the horizon when he
finished. Heaving a satisfied sigh, he straightened his pants
and moved out toward the roadway. He watched as the
cloud grew until it framed a team of horses and, behind
them, the dark, reddish silhouette of a massive coach. A
smile flicked across his face. Soon!

Across the road was a rotting, half-burned shack. Before it stood a pole topped by a weathervane and a

7

sun-bleached rag hanging limply in the heat. Juan crossed to the pole and waited.

The stage was coming on rapidly now, surging out of the desert with the sound of leather slapping and the low drumbeat of hooves. It was an enormous carriage, bigger than any he had ever seen, and it moved with sure, swift grace over the hard ground.

He stepped forward and waved his arm. His yellowed teeth flashed his most ingratiating, most humble smile. Wreathed in sunlight, the horses and coach hurtled down at him.

And swept right past.

Juan spat out fine grit and wiped a film of white dust from his sweaty face. Cursing silently he bent to pick up his sombrero, even grimier now. A twinge of anxiety tightened his stomach. What would happen now that he had missed the stage?

But he hadn't. Braces groaning and squealing, the stage rumbled to a halt fifty yards down the road. Instantly, the coachman clambered down and pulled the horses toward a crude watering trough made of stone. A thin man carrying a rifle got down with him.

Juan admired the waxed paneling of the coach and the burnished lanterns atop it as he approached. The stage was not only immense, nearly as large in fact as the tiny shack in which he had been born, but it was elegantly and elaborately finished as well. Drawn white curtains concealed the interior from his view.

Two rifle-bearing guards seated on the roof peered down suspiciously at him. Juan removed his sombrero, beamed at them, and shuffled toward the coachman.

"*Señor* . . ." he called.

The man ignored him. His practiced hands roved deftly over harnesses and buckles, making adjustments, tightening leather.

Juan tried again. "*Señor*," he said meekly. "I must go to San Felipe. . . ."

The coachman glanced up. His face was sunburned and leathered. He stared dully at the beefy Mexican with oily hair and dirty farmer's clothes standing in the roadway, hat in hand, then looked past him.

"Straight ahead!" He pointed at the horizon. "About eighty miles."

"Really, señor . . . I was thinking . . ." Juan nodded timidly toward the stage.

The coachman's brows darted up in amusement. "Thinking what?"

"I have the money, señor." Juan groped in his pocket and dug out a handful of grimy banknotes and coins.

The coachman exchanged a surprised look with the guards. Doubt registered in his face when he turned back. Clearly, he found it perplexing that this unshaven, greasy peon had come by so much money. Juan shifted his feet. For some reason, an image of the ants floundering in his water swam to mind. These gringos were as predictable as ants.

The coachman's face softened suddenly into a grin. "Hey, boys. This one wants a ride." He laughed. "And he's even got the dinero."

His eyes raked Juan. "Betcha got a few lice and fleas too, huh?" He seemed to like the idea.

Juan grimaced noncommittally. The coachman was delighted.

"I think maybe we oughta let our friend and his bugs here join our passengers. They could use some of that kind of company."

The others chortled. "I'd like to see their faces when they see him," a pockmarked guard said. He looked about as intelligent as a suitcase.

Saying nothing, Juan moved toward the stagecoach door, remembering to throw his weight heavily from hip to hip and to keep his arms limp at his sides, like a plodding peon. It wasn't enough.

The coachman's hand shot out and stopped him. "Just a minute!"

The hand gripped a leather cord around Juan's neck and pulled.

A flat amulet painted with crude symbols emerged from Juan's shirt. The coachman studied it quizzically.

"It is for ringworm," Juan breathed. A timid grin was back on his face. The man's hand was heavy on his chest and the cord was biting into his neck.

The coachman pulled the cord a little higher. He was smirking now. A small pouch surfaced.

"For measles . . ." Juan explained.

The hand began tugging even faster. A chain of scapulars, amulets, pouches, and charms surfaced from beneath the shirt.

"For mumps . . ." Juan offered.

"The pox . . .

"Scabies . . .

"Syphilis . . ."

They were all laughing.

Juan smiled sheepishly. The air was still and the hot sun beat down on him.

Suddenly, the coachman's hand stopped. His strong fingers groped through the coarse material at something resting on Juan's stomach. The laughter ceased.

"And this knife?" His breath reeked of sour tobacco. "What's that for? Constipation?"

Juan slowly and carefully unbuttoned his shirt. He sucked in his bulging stomach and hauled a long object from under his belt. One of the guards leveled a gun at his head as he did.

He held the object aloft. A thin knife made of soft tin and embedded in a flaming tin heart glinted in the sun. "This is for *everything*," he said. His eyes rolled heavenward. "The Sacred Heart of Jesus . . ."

He held his breath and waited.

The coachman relaxed. "Okay *muchacho*," he said. "Close your shirt and go on up."

Juan opened the door and swung his bulk upward, noting with pleasure the surprise that flickered across the coachman's eyes as they caught the grace and ease of his movements. It was a pleasure he had known before.

He nearly staggered back in surprise. The interior of the coach was more spacious and sumptuous even than the burnished exterior had hinted. Plush red velvet seats, downy curtains, and brocaded wall coverings created the air of a luxurious and elegant salon. Gold-plated handles, grips and hat hooks, ornately finished, studded the walls. The flooring was of soft, thick wool.

A portable table had been set up in the middle of the coach and five people were bent over it, eating hungrily. They were sucking food into already overstuffed mouths and washing it down with wine poured from sleek bottles. On the table and seats lay several leather satchels, their flaps open to reveal still more food and bottles.

A fat cleric had just pulled a greasy chicken from his satchel and was offering it around when the slam of the door made them all look up. They recoiled almost in unison.

Juan noted from the shape of the cleric's dark hat and the splendid sheen of his frock that the man was a monsignor. Jewels glittered on his pudgy fingers, and the flesh of his face was soft and very white for a Mexican.

He looked at him in disgust. A priest for the *aristocracia,* he thought. One of those pampered prelates who had forgotten that their magnificent God had been a tough peon.

There were three Americans. One of them raised a hard, arrogant face. His hair was expertly trimmed and combed and he wore a rich serge suit, closely buttoned. His whole bearing radiated a peculiar luxury and ease, an air of accepted wealth, like that of the absentee landlords Juan had known.

"Well, I'll be goddamned!" the man bellowed. His upper lips curled momentarily in disdain, then he settled back and stared.

A slim, strikingly pretty girl in a gold dress molded tightly around her shoulders and breasts leaned toward the man and whispered in his ear. Dark, sensuous eyes bored into Juan as her lips moved. He noted with pleasure that she was much younger than the American.

"Never mind, dear," the man said, patting her hand reassuringly.

With a start, the coach lurched forward, throwing them all off balance. Juan straightened himself and removed his hat, holding it respectfully before him. He scanned the others.

The third American had a soft, mottled face and dark lines under his eyes. His wide-brimmed hat was shabby and his tan wastecoat bulged carelessly over a burly frame. There was a restrained, almost tightly leashed, nervousness in his expression, and a suggestion of stealth in his bloodless lips. Juan guessed that he was a salesman, one of those *bastardo* peddlers from the American South with their cheap gadgets and phony *simpatía* for Mexican peasants. He felt a momentary flare of irritation, then dismissed it, and the American, as trivial.

There was no question about the last passenger, the one seated in the far corner licking tortilla crumbs from his manicured fingers. The lace on his shirt and the elegant trim of his moustache marked him as assuredly as his smooth Castillian features. Pure *castelano!* No Indian blood whatever. Only one thing marred his patrician bearing: his skin. It was strangely sallow, almost yellow. Jaundice!

Juan regarded him with detachment. Except for the brief flaring of his nostrils at the sight of Juan, the man betrayed nothing. He looked away and reached for some wine. His aloofness was as predictable as nightfall. The mejicano *noble* to perfection. Underneath, he would be a pig.

It was becoming difficult to stand in the swaying coach. Juan glanced at the nearest empty seat and moved shyly toward it.

A large white hat plopped down in front of him.

The rich-looking American had reached casually above his head, plucked the hat from its hook and tossed it on the seat. His lips were edged into a thin, challenging smile. No one spoke.

Juan nodded humbly and turned toward another seat. With an air of indifference, the American stretched his legs and planted them across the seat. His boots were of rich, tooled leather.

"Where you going?" he said.

Juan stiffened. It wasn't a question. It was an assertion of dominance. He could either knock it down or submit.

He shrugged abjectly.

The American glared at him and shook his head. Beside him, the pretty wife stirred uneasily. The man pointed to the farthest corner of the coach.

"Over there!"

Obediently, Juan shuffled toward an apparently smooth wall. Gold cloth set in polished wood faced him. Halfway down, concealed in the woodwork, was a gold handle.

"Pull it!" the man ordered.

He reached out and tugged, stumbling backwards as he did. A door glided open with surprising ease.

The sight startled him. A small but apparently workable bathroom stood before him. The toilet gleamed like a polished stone. Next to it was a basin and, above that, a gilt-edged mirror. In all details the compact room was as luxuriously appointed as the rest of the coach.

Behind him they were all chuckling.

The muscles in his shoulders tensed and his stomach went hard. He consciously suppressed the balling of his fists and closed the door softly, comforted in a way by the crassness of the American. He knew what such behavior concealed.

He turned around and held out his hands in a gesture of helplessness. The American nodded toward the wall. "The other one," he said.

There was another handle in the wall, not far from the one to the bathroom door. Cautiously, Juan pulled it.

The wall gave way and a small seat folded outward. It was intriguing, so clever. Juan sat down.

"I guess he understands English," the American said. "He just doesn't like to talk."

The monsignor stopped chewing on a thick beef rib. "Now, now," he admonished. "Even peasants are—"

He broke off abruptly and extended the rib toward the woman, who was fishing in one of the leather satchels. "Some mustard please," he said. "Thank you."

"As I was saying . . . " He was chewing furiously now and his words were thick and garbled. "Even *they* are people. They too . . . have rights. After all, they have . . . just won a . . . revolution. . . ."

Across from him the Mexican *noble* bit into a chicken leg. *"Brutos* . . ." he muttered. "Animals!" He belched.

Juan was watching the woman. Her movements as she buttered a piece of toast were refined, almost dainty. She seemed intent on her meal but her eyes kept stealing glances at him. There was a hint of fascination in them.

"Yes, animals . . ." she repeated, automatically. "I wonder if he has crabs?"

Juan considered scratching. Instead, obligingly, he picked his nose.

The monsignor was off on another tack. A new thought had struck him. "You should hear them in the confessional; the things they confess . . ." he said. His hand slid toward a canape. "Do you know what they——"

The woman cut him off. "Oh, I can imagine, Father, I can imagine. I mean, they live in such promiscuity. All of them in one room. At night. With the lights out. You

never know who's next: mother, sister, daughter, goat.
. . ."

Juan said nothing. This woman had possibilities.

The salesman type muttered something about "niggers."
They were all caught up in the game now.

"Just like animals," the *noble* spat. Wine dribbled down
his chin and onto his suit.

"Hey, you!" the rich-looking American barked. "You
ever know your father?"

Juan was sitting immobile in his corner, his face impassive. Now he gave a vague, embarrassed grimace.

"How many kids you got?"

He shrugged. Who knows?

"Sheeeit," the American said. "And that imbecile Madero, that dumb excuse for a President, wanted to give
our land to people like this."

So the man was a landlord.

"Fortunately," the monsignor said. "Divine providence
has rid us of Francisco Madero." He slurped at a creamy
pudding which Juan did not recognize.

"It wasn't providence," the landowner sneered. He tore
a hunk of meat from a leg of roasted lamb. "It was General Huerta. Thank God for him. He put these people in
their places."

They were all busily eating now. Grease smeared their
faces and crumbs stuck to their clothes. They kept talking
as they chewed, spilling out bits of food and drops of
liquid, which splattered about. Juan savored the sight.

He was still sitting with a mindless grin frozen on his
face, his eyes blank, thinking that it would not be long
now, when the stage thumped to a halt.

Chapter Two

They had been rolling along for more than an hour toward the foothills of the Sierras. Gradually, the terrain began to change. Small patches of green could be seen and, in the near distance, more trees.

The horses pulled at a steady gait, only beginning to show the first signs of weariness. They had run hard that morning and still had the hills to negotiate, but as the coachman was anxious to escape the desert heat, he lashed them on.

They came round a corner bordering a pond, the first they had seen all day, and before them the road slanted steeply upward. The horses took the first hundred yards at a run, then began to slow. A moment later the team was moving at a walk, straining against the braces.

Near the crest their feet began to slip. The whip cracked relentlessly against their flesh, the coachman screaming, "Hyaaah! Hyaaah!" shrilly. The stage inched forward.

At the side of the road, the coachman noticed now, several Mexicans, perhaps ten, sat in the shade of a dilapidated old cart, their sombreros over their eyes. Siesta. Most of them were children but even they looked to be sturdy little peons. Odd that they were there; but as they were, they could be useful.

"Hey, you!" the coachman called in Spanish. "Hey, give us a hand. We need a push."

No one moved.

The coachman flayed the straining horses. "Come on, now," he shouted. "Give us a push."

The Mexicans slumbered on.

"Shit! Those lazy bastards never move their asses." He screamed again at the horses, and they trudged slowly past the cart and out of sight around a ridge.

When the stage disappeared, the Mexicans sprang up and darted after it, keeping hidden behind the ridge. Unseen, two boys dashed out to the road and quickly wedged blocks of wood under the slipping rear wheels. Then they faded back into the roadside.

The stage was stuck now. Frantically, the coachman lashed at the horses. To no avail. On the sharp incline, five thousand pounds was too much of a burden to haul over the wood.

On their bellies now, the two boys slithered under the front of the stage. They held large, heavy knives. They rolled onto their backs and began hacking at the taut leather straps inches above their faces. One parted, then another, then with a sharp snap the last brace gave.

Freed suddenly, the horses tottered forward and broke into a run. A terrifying scream, the scream of a man in abject panic, rent the air. With the reins still wrapped tightly around his hands, the coachman plummeted earthward, pulled by the unleashed horses. His body hit the ground with a dull plop and his screams died out instantly. He was dragged another fifty yards before the reins unravelled from his hands.

Atop the stage, the three guards swung desperately around, guns level. Nothing. Then the bushes rustled and a boy who looked no more than sixteen stepped onto the road. An old, single-shot carbine was slung under his arm.

"Put your guns down and notheeng will happen to you," he said in English. His accent was heavy.

As a man, the guards turned to shoot him. The boy never moved. He didn't have to. A volley from unseen guns cut the guards down before they got off a shot. "*Estúpido,*" the boy muttered.

Inside the coach Juan sat impassive on his small seat, watching the others. At the coachman's scream they started up in alarm. "What the hell—" the American landowner said. His wife clutched his arm.

"Oh, God!" she gasped. "That was awful!"

They looked about them confusedly. The monsignor shrank back against his seat, groping for a cross.

The sound of the shots contorted their faces in fear. "*Los insurrectos!*" the *noble* cried. "The rebels!" His jaundiced face had gone white.

They froze at the word. A spasm shook the jellied body of the monsignor. In the corner, the man who looked like a salesman began to whimper.

A moment later the white curtains parted violently. Rifles and shotguns suddenly were thrust through the windows.

Behind the level gun barrels, peering into the coach, appeared the faces of grinning peons. Save for one, they were the faces of boys. Each was dark, with a blunt chin setting off an oval face. They looked very much alike. The youngest appeared to be no more than ten or eleven.

The only man was old, very old, with the soft, weathered skin and sorrowful eyes of the Mexican peasant. He too was grinning.

The *noble* relaxed visibly at the sight of the peons. Juan saw his scrawny hand steal quickly toward the inside of his jacket. The butt of a short-barreled revolver emerged.

The youngest boy was at the window nearest Juan, his hands encasing an enormous shotgun. The barrel was pointed at the *noble,* but the boy was looking elsewhere, staring in fascination at the shuddering monsignor.

Without rising, Juan leaned toward the boy. His hands encircled the boy's and his massive finger forced the small finger back against the trigger. The shotgun crashed loudly.

The impact threw the boy backward. A scream exploded from the woman, a long, fearful cry that made her husband grab her violently and pull her, trembling, against him.

Across from her, almost within reach, a gaping hole appeared in the chest of the *noble*. Blood spurted from it. The man's eyes stared glassily for a moment at the blood, then up at Juan. Juan smiled. The man slumped down in the velvet seat. He was dead.

Juan rose and opened the door. Several boys clambered into the carriage, jostling one another and taking fake pot shots at the cowering passengers. The passengers sat stunned, staring stupidly at Juan. He regarded them with amusement. Instead of the heavy, sodden peasant, he knew he suddenly appeared to them to be immense and formidable. He knew his own face, too: When he wasn't acting the sleepy, humble peon, it was hard and cunning.

"Throw him out," he said, pointing to the *noble*. "He'll mess up the furniture."

The youngest boy looked at him. "We kill them all, okay, Pa?" he said. As if in assertion of his power to do it, he fired his shotgun in the direction of the monsignor, blowing a hole in the window curtain.

Juan smacked him. The boy's eyes watered and his mouth curled in pain, but he gave no cry.

"Chulo, you are an idiot," Juan said. "You do not shoot unless Papa pulls the trigger. You are too young. You understand?"

He glanced at the sweating, trembling passengers and felt a flush of delight at their baffled expressions. "These are my kids," he explained. "You treat them nice. You give them all the money you got. *Comprende?*" He pointed at the quivering monsignor. "And you, padre, those rings from your fingers. Okay?"

He remembered something then. He crossed to the landowner and seized the flesh of his cheek, squeezing brutally until it was red. The man looked up helplessly. His wife moaned beside him.

Juan put his face down to the American's. "You asked about my family, didn't you?" he breathed. "How many kids I got? Here . . ." His free hands swept the air. "Count them!

"The little one," Juan said, "that's Chulo. Those two, Pepe and Napolean, they're twins. That one with the old gun, that's Benito. A good boy. Likes the girls. That's Nene. He's a good boy. And that's the oldest, Sebastian. He drinks too much but he's okay."

He pointed to the open door. "Those are my men out there." Three men could be seen watching the coach. "That's Fefe, that's Amando, that's Pancho."

The American sucked in his breath. It was suddenly very quiet in the coach.

"And you wanted to know if I knew my father." Juan reached out and pulled the old man toward him. "Here, say hello. His name's Nino." The American nodded toward the old man. "At least he *says* he's my father," Juan laughed. "But I believe him."

Nino grinned toothlessly.

Juan let go the man's cheek and slapped him heartily on the shoulder. "Okay?" he said. "You be nice from now on to dumb Mexicans. Right?"

The American nodded silently but remained tense and hesitant. Juan studied the man. The certainty of what would happen overwhelmed him. The American would abuse the first dumb, weak mejicano he met; he would need the vindication. Juan's mouth tasted sour. The man was hopeless. Or was he?

"By the way," Juan said softly. "How many children you got?" He looked at the wife as he spoke.

The landowner shrank back and stammered, "I, uh . . . we . . . uh . . ."

Juan shook his head sadly. "Don't worry," he said.

"That can be fixed." He patted the American solicitously on the back.

He reached out suddenly and grabbed the wife and pulled her to her feet. Her dress rustled noisily in the quiet coach. She looked anxiously at her husband, too confused and frightened to say anything. Her mouth dropped but no sound came out.

Juan pulled her toward the door. She hung back, casting desperate looks around, until the old man, Nino, prodded her in the rear with the stock of his rifle.

"*Andale!*" he ordered.

Hesitantly, she allowed herself to be dragged along behind Juan. Her wrist felt cool in his hand. He noticed his sons watching in amusement.

"Where is he taking her?" the American whined. "What's he gonna do to her?"

"You ain't figured it out yet?" the old man replied.

They dismounted the stage. The sun was bright, almost dazzling, and the air was dry and still.

"Where are we going?" the woman asked. Her voice was tiny and afraid. Juan didn't answer.

He pulled her off the road and through some bushes. The leaves raked his face and left an air of mint in his nose. He liked the woman's perfume better.

He left her standing in a bush near the edge of the road. He noticed that her fists were balled and that in the shade she looked even prettier than she had in the stage, darker and more sensual. Her expression was forlorn but her eyes still burned into him, making a lie of all the rest. He hoped that she would resist just a little. For the sport of it.

He found what he wanted ten feet the other side of a thick cluster of bushes: a tree standing in a mossy clearing. Through an opening in the bushes the woman was clearly visible. Juan whistled, as to a dog, and just as obediently the woman came toward him, taking small, timid steps.

Juan reached for her, ignoring the terrified look she

suddenly flashed. He grasped her by the shoulders and as easily as if she were a doll, propped her against the tree. His grimy hands flew up to her breasts and curled around the gold dress.

"Oh, no," she gasped. "No." Good, she was resisting. Not enough to be convincing—but enough.

Under his hands her flesh was firm but the starched, crinolined dress material was irritating. Juan reached down and threw up her skirt, discovering smooth stocking and garters and, to his delight, soft thighs. His fingers probed under the garters.

"Oh, Jesus," the woman moaned. "Oh, God, I'll faint."

"You gonna miss the best part if you faint," he said, and tore open the front of her dress.

Her breasts tumbled out. Juan held her at arm's length and looked down at them. They were very white. A shadow from a branch above slashed across her breasts, muting the pink tips. Juan leaned toward her.

Her eyes were aglow now and her mouth hung half open. A pained looked suddenly twisted across her face and her nostrils flared. The look made him tense in anticipation: he knew it well. Still, she managed to surprise him.

Before he could react, the woman's hands shot out and grabbed his pants at the waist. With frenzied strength, she pulled violently downward. The shabby material gave. Buttons dropped to the ground.

Juan felt a breath of cool air whisk across his bare buttocks. Sounds of whooping and laughter reached him from the coach as he and the woman tumbled to the ground in a sweating, thrashing heap. He thought briefly of her husband, then abandoned himself to the role of stud. He hoped it was her time. She deserved the moment o.

She was being very good.

Chapter Three

Juan's boys stripped the passengers down to their underwear. All but the one who looked like a salesman. "I'm an American," he protested. "I'm a citizen of the United States. You can't do this to me."

Him they made strip naked.

They pushed the men from the coach and went through the passengers' clothing, emptying the pockets. Then they rifled the baggage. One of the landowner's shirts appealed to Sebastian and he pulled it on, stuffing his own torn and greasy shirt into the man's rucksack. Napolean appropriated a belt and vest from the other American. Old man Nino spurned a challenge to put on the monsignor's frock. Then they tossed some pants out to the passengers and waited for Juan.

Juan tied his torn trousers together as best he could. He fumbled with the few remaining buttons, watching the woman seated silently on the ground before him. She was langorously combing her hair, taking slow, thoughtful strokes. Her dress was held together with hairclips.

Finished, Juan called to her. "Adelita."

Startled and apprehensive, she looked up at him. His huge, calloused hand was extended toward her. "Your hand," he said.

She hesitated, then flashed him a languid smile and held out her hand. Juan took it. It was cool and delicate. Juan caught a sudden, sensual appeal in her eyes. He beamed at her and slid two rings off her fingers.

She jerked her hand free in outrage. *"Gracias,"* Juan said.

The boys were already at the wine when they returned to the coach. Juan came up behind little Chulo, who seemed determined to outdo his brothers, and plucked the bottle from his mouth. "Later," he said, and cuffed the boy affectionately on the head.

The passengers were herded into the old mule cart on the side of the road and the still unconscious coachman was lowered into the back. The landowner stared imploringly at his wife all the while, but she looked away in icy indifference. When he tried to put a comforting arm around her, she slapped him resoundingly. Chulo giggled at the sight. "Why is she angry with him, Papa?" he said. "Because he didn't protect her from you?"

"No, *niño*. Because he isn't me."

The monsignor was still trembling when Juan handed him the reigns. "You should have no trouble, padre," Juan said. "You are used to being nice to asses."

He slapped the nearest mule and the cart inched forward. "Have a nice trip." He glanced amiably at the woman but she averted her eyes. The cart moved slowly up the hill and out of sight.

"Hey, Fefe," Juan called to one of his men. "Go find the horses for the stage. Okay? Hurry."

The sound of distant explosions suddenly brought his head up sharply. The explosions had the timbre of gattling fire but were more uneven, with a hollow ring. He stared curiously into the distance. A small dust cloud was visible on the horizon.

Juan snapped his fingers and held out his hand. Napolean understood immediately and placed a spyglass in it. Unconsciously, Juan reached into his pocket for something to clean the lens.

"Oh, weeeeeee. Weeeeeee."

Chulo was squeeling. The others were cackling and slapping each other's backs. Juan looked down at his hand. In it were the woman's panties, soft white things edged in lace. He wiped the lens with them and casually tossed the garment over his shoulder to the ground.

The glass revealed a tiny figure astride a metallic machine with two wheels. The figure was bent over the handlebars, head up, and was guiding the machine swiftly and deftly along the curving road. His body rose gracefully with each bump and his arms seemed to absorb the impact as if they were springs. Juan watched in curiosity and admiration. So that was a motorcycle. But what the hell was it doing out here?

The machine rounded a bend and disappeared behind a hill. Juan lowered the glass and shrugged. If he waits long enough, he thought, a man finds out everything he has to in life. Maybe he'd find out about the machine.

They hitched the horses to the coach when Fefe returned with them an hour later. Old man Nino, an old stagehand, spliced the straps together with some leather thongs, braiding them rapidly in an expert handweave that fascinated the *muchachos*. Then, against his will, he obeyed Juan's order to climb up and take the reins.

"Hey, Papa. I ride inside with you, okay?" Chulo implored.

"You all ride inside with me. The men can ride on the roof."

Napolean grimaced. "That means I have to ride on the roof, huh?" Napolean was fifteen.

"You? Who says you're a man," Juan chided. "If you were a man you would've said, 'Me first!' when I grabbed that woman. No, you ride inside."

An hour later they were winding through the mountains, past outcroppings of jagged rock set against a bleak and barren terrain. The air was cooler than it had been on the desert floor, not much but enough to make for a pleasant ride.

Juan was sprawled on one of the seats inside. The velvet felt soft and reassuring under him. He watched his sons hungrily tear into the food left behind by the former passengers. Wine ran in a meandering stream down the shirtfront of Benito, the second youngest at fourteen, and his eyes already looked glazed and far away. He kept insisting, with a silly expression, that he wasn't drunk. The others just as insistently urged more wine on him.

Juan lit a cigar and studied it in satisfaction. Napolean had liberated it from the body of the *noble*. It tasted only slightly stale. No matter.

He looked around him. His eyes fondled every crevice of the coach, made love to the filagreed gold fixtures, ran blissfully over the hand-tooled door coverings, reveled in the texture of the flooring. Ay, yes, they had done a splendid job for him.

Chulo pulled a dirty finger out of his nose and wiped it on the upholstery. Enraged, Juan lurched up and slapped him. Quickly, he cleaned the offending spot with his sleeve. "From now on," he snapped, "this is our house." He kicked out hard and knocked Sebastian's feet off one of the seats.

Juan grabbed a bottle of wine from Sebastian and leaned out the window. Nino was driving with a determined set to his face. His jaw muscles bulged under the wrinkled skin and his lips were pursed in a near snarl.

"Hey, old man."

"Yeah?"

"Wanna drink?"

The old man made a vulgar gesture. He started to say something but was suddenly cut short by a loud explosion that made him grab in shock at the reins. The sound was loud and nearby, much louder than a gun blast.

"What the hell—?" Juan gripped tightly to the doorframe. A coughing, sputtering bark followed the blast and was in turn succeeded by the same sharp pops they had heard in the distance earlier. Only now the explosions were close, very close.

"Stop!" he screamed up at Nino. "Stop this thing!"

The stage jolted to a halt. Juan threw open the door and leaped out, trailed by his sons. He peered down the road. They were in a narrow canyon. A dust cloud from off the plain was swirling through the pass, blocking his view of the road ahead. Juan stood dumbfounded, listening to the approaching backfire of the motorcycle.

Then suddenly, before he could brace himself, the machine roared out of the cloud. Juan had a sudden vision of a lean figure draped in a long black overcoat down to the ankles with an inner tube slung over one shoulder before he was nearly knocked to the ground. The black coat and the inner tube swept within inches of him, and he saw that atop them sat a bowler hat from under which flowed long blond hair. The face between the hat and the coat wore an imperturbable expression, a look oblivious to the men and boys standing in the roadway.

The machine twisted through them like a snake after a lizard and sped past the stage. Juan cursed silently and reached for his pistol. He wasn't wearing one. He jabbed Pepe, who was standing near him, and the boy turned just enough to let Juan pull a pistol from his grip. Quickly, he sighted down the road and fired.

The motorcycle swerved, nearly tipped over, then slid to a halt.

The man atop it casually dismounted, without even looking around. He bent down and studied the rear tire, which was flat, and unslung the inner tube. He seemed about as disturbed as he would have been had he run over a sharp rock.

Juan regarded him with interest. The man was thirty, forty feet away but he might have been alone in the desert for all the awareness he showed of the clutch of people staring at him. Curious! The length and color of the man's hair suggested he was European (Americans wore their hair shorter), and the bowler only served to confirm it. But what was he doing here?

The man glanced up at him for the first time. His face

was composed, almost serene in its coolness. The features were angular, not sharp at all but firm and direct. The face of a man who was sure of himself. Juan wondered if the man could kill, and his fingers tightened unconsciously on the pistol.

The dust was settling, raining softly down around them all. Juan stared through it at black coat and bowler, who sighed and began walking toward him. He held the inner tube in one hand.

Black coat, bowler, and impervious face drew closer. Juan chewed nonchalantly on his lighted cigar but watched the man warily. The black coat stopped a foot away. Cool eyes studied him. A hand came slowly up and tunneled inside the black coat, making Juan tense. The hand emerged holding a small white cylinder. A cigarette?

"Got a light?" the man said.

His voice was relaxed and easy, beguilingly so. The man's Spanish was good but curiously accented. Juan had heard the accent just once before. Irish!

He started to answer but the man cut him off with a courteous wave of the hand. Just as politely, the Irishman reached up and eased Juan's cigar from his mouth. His movements were so slow and casual as to be unthreatening. He pressed the burning end of the cigar against the cylinder, then stuck the cigar back in Juan's mouth.

Stunned by it all, Juan stood dead still. He would thrash the Irishman if necessary, he thought, but at the moment he was overcome by the man's style. He watched as the Irishman neatly flipped the cylinder in the direction of the coach instead of smoking it. What the hell was going on?

The cylinder landed on the carriage roof. The Irishman moved with sudden and surprising speed toward the coach. Chulo, sitting on the running board, gazed up at him, transfixed. The Irishman grabbed his arm and gently but firmly pulled the boy off his seat and away from the stagecoach. Juan watched the man and the boy slide rapidly toward him, then heard the Irishman's calm voice.

"Duck, you sucker!" the voice said.

The air shook and Juan's ears rang with a hard crash that sounded like a gun going off in his ear. He dove to the ground with the others. Flames flashed momentarily atop the stagecoach and then gave way to a small black cloud that seemed to congeal upon itself and then spurt upward. A wispy trail of gray smoke followed.

Unbelieving, Juan bolted up and ran toward the stage. He pulled open the door and peered inside. Through a ragged hole in the roof he could see the high blue sky. The wood was charred, and a black ring circled the hole, staining the satiny coach ceiling.

Rage gripped him. He wheeled and pointed his pistol at the Irishman, cocking it as he did. It struck him that he was being stupid, but he didn't care. His finger tightened on the trigger.

Incredibly, the Irishman merely arched his eyebrows and shook his head in admonishment at the sight of the gun, as to a naughty child. Juan paused.

"Tch . . . tch. . . ." The Irishman was actually clucking.

There was a frozen moment in which everything seemed to await some cosmic event. Juan wondered why he didn't shoot the cocky bastard, and the mere fact of his thinking about it stayed his finger on the trigger. In that moment, the Irishman unhooked a flask hanging from his shoulder, one of two small, identical flasks Juan hadn't noticed before. He unscrewed the top.

"I wouldn't shoot if I were you," he said.

From the top of the flask hung an appendage resembling an eye dropper. The Irishman held it as far from his body as possible and turned the nose down. "If you shoot, I might fall," he said. A smiled played at the corners of his mouth.

A drop collected at the tip of the eyedropper; it swelled

and unloosed itself. Juan's eyes followed it downward. The drop took about two days to hit the ground.

It hit with an explosion that banged against Juan's eardrums and made his *niños* jump back in alarm. On the ground a vapor cloud went from black to gray to white. The smoke cleared to reveal a hole as large as a sombrero.

The Irishman seemed unperturbed. He said, "If you shoot me and I fall, they'll have to make new maps. Because when I go half of Mexico goes with me. Look!"

He unbuttoned his black overcoat and held it open. The inside was lined on both sides with pockets from which bulged sticks of dynamite, detonators, and fuses. There were also more flasks, filled, Juan assumed, like the others—with nitroglycerin. In all, the Irishman carried enough explosives to destroy all of Cherudado, where Juan was born, and the twenty other villages in the same valley.

Speechless, Juan let his hand relax on the pistol. He stared in mute fascination at the Irishman, then down at the hole. A new emotion suddenly washed over him. The whole of his life stopped at that moment. His years as a farmer, a cowboy, a bartender, as a pimp and a bandit congealed into one overwhelming vision. The vision even had a name.

He was aware that he was smiling strangely. His children and his men, even old Nino, were staring at him in astonishment. Even the Irishman looked perplexed. Juan didn't care. For the first time in years, perhaps since his days under the scalding sun in the fields, his mind was uncluttered with schemes and calculations. Now only one scheme held him.

"Something wrong?" the Irishman was saying.

Juan showed his toothiest smile and slid his pistol into his pants. "I was just thinking that we were even," he said.

"Not yet. You're going to give me a ride now."

The Irishman walked toward the coach. He flipped the

spare tube at Chulo as he passed the boy. "And you, monkey, are going to fix that tire." His tone left no room for refusal.

Juan let the Irishman pass him and climb into the coach. In disbelief, Chulo charged at him and grabbed his sleeve. "Shoot him, Papa!" he screamed. "When he sits down, you shoot him in the mouth. Okay, Papa?"

Poor Chulo! He didn't understand. He had never before seen his father bested by another man, except when for one reason or another he was playacting. The boy was stunned and confused now. He could remain confused. In time, a man learns everything he has to.

"Go fix the tire!" Juan barked, and slapped at Chulo's head.

The Irishman was already sprawled across a divan when Juan hauled himself up. A flask was in his mouth and he was drinking deeply from it. Juan started back and his muscles instinctively tensed in anticipation of disaster. He realized that the flask contained only whisky a fraction before the Irishman held up its lethal mate to show him. Juan uncoiled.

"Where are you going in this buggy?" the Irishman asked. He pulled at his flask.

"Ahhhhh . . . where you going?"

"The silver mines."

"At Lucainena?" The Irishman nodded. "Ah, yes, Mr. Aschenbach, the German, runs them. I know him. Nice stuff he's got."

The Irishman's head bobbed in agreement. He tilted the flask to his mouth again.

"Why you going there?"

There was no answer. The Irishman drained the flask and let it fall to the seat beside him, then lowered his hat over his eyes.

"Hey, Firecracker," Juan called. No answer. Juan stuck his cigar in his mouth and bent toward the man. He raised the Irishman's hat. The man seemed to be asleep. With a shrug, Juan replaced the hat and backed toward the door. Nino and Fefe were standing there, peering in. "Put a wick in his mouth and he'll light up for a month," he said to them, chuckling, then felt his stomach tighten as he realized how close to the Irishman his burning cigar had been.

His *niños* were swarming like jackals around a fiber suitcase tied to the back of the Irishman's machine. Juan chased them with a few kicks in the rear and opened the suitcase himself.

Lying flat across the top, neatly folded, was a large green cloth. Juan held it up. The letters IRA were sewed evenly onto the material. A flag? If it was a flag, it was like none he had ever seen. He crumbled it and tossed it to the ground.

Another object caught his eye, a piece of yellowing paper covered with large block letters, including, in English, the word WANTED. The paper was thin and had the texture of newsprint. Juan unfolded it. A photograph of the Irishman stared up at him. Under it was a notice that the British government was offering three hundred pounds for the capture of one John Mallory, described as a "dangerous terrorist."

"Good for you, Firecracker," Juan muttered to himself. He put the clipping in his pocket.

The remaining contents of the suitcase didn't surprise him, except in quantity. Dynamite, pyrite, bottles of acid, more fuses, timing mechanisms, small wooden detonators. The Irishman could mine a great deal of silver with that, if that were his intention. Juan wondered how many British he had killed.

"Shit! Not even one peso," Napolean said.

Juan smiled at the boy. "You aren't seeing right, *muchacho*," he said. "This suitcase is a bank."

"A bank? If that's a bank I'm Pancho Villa!"

"You're smarter than Villa, but not as smart as your Papa."

His sons looked at him in bewilderment. Only Niño showed any comprehension. The old man began wheezing in alarm. An appalled whisper escaped him. "Mesa Verde! The bank . . . !"

"Hey, now you understand," Juan said. "Mesa Verde. El Banco Nacionale de Mesa Verde." That was the name of his vision. "That suitcase and Firecracker, they're gonna make us rich."

Somewhere nearby some crickets were heralding the setting of the sun. For long moments no other sound could be heard.

Fefe finally broke the silence. "Who needs Firecracker," he grumbled. "All we need is matches and guts, and I got both."

Juan frowned. Fefe was a southerner with flat features and small, almost beady eyes. His cheekbones were high, like his Indian ancestors, but he lacked the Indian cunning and their faith that life was most intelligently lived by letting others do the hard work. Too much Spanish blood, Juan thought; it weakened the brain. Too many of Fefe's people forced to grovel on some *noble's* cropland had diluted a wise heritage. Fefe shouldn't be so arrogant; he wasn't smart enough.

"No, *amigo*," he said. "We need an expert."

"Hah. For what? To light a match?"

"Yes, to light a match."

Juan turned to Benito, grabbed the poncho from the boy's shoulder and thrust it at Fefe.

"Here, go cover Irish. He might catch cold."

Fefe gathered the poncho sourly to him and walked away. Juan watched him go. Too bad Fefe wasn't an expert. Too bad none of them were. Now he would have to find a way to persuade Irish to cooperate in a supposedly impossible task. No one had ever succeeded in robbing the Mesa Verde Bank. Too many guards. Too many precautions. And now all those soldiers would be bolstering the guard because the government feared those fool revolutionaries.

But with Irish they could do it. He, Juan, knew just how.

Chapter Four

They rode for several hours deeper into the Sierras. The evening air came down pale and cool, and a pink sun squatted on the horizon, reluctant to go. They pulled off the road and rumbled a few miles along a dry stream bed, then through a thicket and into a narrow gorge invisible from all directions. Mallory, the Irishman, slept through it all.

They pulled out two of the coach seats and replaced the one under the hole in the roof with an iron stove. The stovepipe poked out through the hole. Between the walls they strung hammocks in a double tier. Nino nailed a shelf to another wall. On the shelf he placed a statue of his patron saint, Frances, and a white vigil candle. Above it, Juan hung a faded picture postcard of a massive building with a lettered portico. The lettering read: BANCO NACIONAL DE MESA VERDE.

A pot of soup was bubbling on the stove when Mallory finally awoke. From outside, where he was eating with the rest of his gang, Juan saw the Irishman bolt up and look about him in confusion. Chulo stuck his head in the window and barked something in a nasty tone that Juan couldn't make out.

Mallory came down from the coach and turned to study it. Smoke curled out of the stovepipe. The Irishman shook his head in admiration and ambled over to Juan.

Juan sat in one of the two red velvet seats taken from the coach and set up beside a small table set for two. He gestured to the empty seat. Mallory ignored him and, still standing, took a piece of meat from the table and bit into it.

"What kind of work do you do for the German?" Juan said. There was no point in wasting time on preliminaries.

"I look for silver lodes."

"With your eyedropper, huh?" Mallory was silent. "You know, that stuff is like holy water," Juan said. He scratched at his beard. "It's a mortal sin to misuse it. And for what? To blow holes in a mountain? To find a piece of silver? And for Aschenbach, that German." He spat contemptuously.

Mallory sat down and took another piece of meat. "You got any better ideas?"

"Yeah. Gold. That's a better idea."

"Forget it. There isn't any around here."

"Sure there is, Firecracker. In Mesa Verde."

A swarm of gnats swam toward the table. Mallory brushed them away and asked, "Isn't that a city?"

"Sure, Irish. Where are the banks where you live, out in the country?"

"Ah, a bank!" Mallory's lean face puckered shrewdly. For the first time, Juan noticed something more than hardness in the Irishman's eyes. Now they flickered in amusement.

"Not a bank. The bank. The richest bank outside of Mexico City, maybe the richest in the country. They've got money sticking out of drawers there. They blow their noses in it, they've got so much money. Right, Nino?"

The old man, squatting nearby, nodded his head.

"I saw the inside of that bank once when I was eight years old," Juan said. "Nino took me in there to look it over the day before he tried to rob it." He turned to the old man. "You remember that?"

"Not too good," Nino said sadly. He looked at Mallory. "They got me as soon as I got inside. They gave me thirty-two years for it. Thirty-two years." His voice choked. "They let me out three months ago."

"That's okay, Nino," Juan boomed. "We're gonna go back and do it right this time. You and me and our friend Firecracker." He looked at the Irishman's impassive face. "Hey, what's your name anyway."

"John."

"Hah, like Juan. The same name."

"So what?"

Hard lines were suddenly edged under Mallory's eyes and along his chin. His long blond hair swayed gently in the breeze but didn't offset the severity of his face: the protruding jaw, the gaunt cheeks, the slashed eyebrows. Juan thought, not without satisfaction, that he would have to watch Irish closely. The man could indeed kill.

"I thought," he said carefully, "that maybe having the same name was destiny."

Mallory got up. "Yeah, well my destiny is the silver mines."

"You don't wanna be my partner? You don't wanna get rich?"

"I only want my motorcycle." He looked around the clearing.

"The hell with your motorcycle. If you want it, it's over there, leaning on the rock." Without looking, Juan pointed across the gorge. "But you don't want it. We got something else to talk about."

"*Where* is it?" Mallory snapped.

Juan turned. There was only an empty space where the machine should have been. His sons stood near the space wearing blank expressions. In a shot he was out of the chair hurtling toward them.

"You lousy sons of bitches." His feet and arms lashed out, sending several of the *niños* sprawling. "Get that goddamn motorcycle."

The fading sun suddenly glinted on a polished knife. Juan jumped back. He felt the cold tip of the blade rake lightly across his skin as it slashed his sleeve from the elbow to the cuff. His hand shot out and grabbed little Chulo by the shirt. He held him at arm's length. Motherofchrist the kid was learning fast. He smiled at Mallory, a boys-will-be-boys smile.

Juan took the knife and pushed Chulo towards his brothers. "Now get it," he said. The boys vanished into the bushes.

They reappeared a few minutes later. Chulo came out carrying the handlebars. Behind him, Benito shouldered the frame. Nene had a wheel and the chain, Sebastian the other wheel. The gas tank was under Napolean's arm. They deposited the parts at Mallory's feet.

It took Mallory an hour to reassemble the machine. Juan watched in dismay, wondering how to stop the Irishman, how to convince him. He paced along the gorge, then went briefly into the coach. The statue caught his eye. Why not? He prayed, his lips moving furiously in supplication. Nothing came to him, no brilliant solutions. He went back outside.

He tried again. "Look, Firecracker. If it's money, I'll give you more than fifty per cent." No answer. Mallory tightened a bolt on the machine. "Come on, you handle the explosives and I'll do all the rest. Okay?" Still no answer. "Listen, we were made for each other. I'm a bandit and you're a bandit."

Mallory looked up in genuine surprise. "What makes you say that?"

Juan reached into his pocket and pulled out the clipping. He waved it in front of Mallory's face.

"Uh, uh, *amigo*," Mallory said. "That's something else. I wasn't a bandit."

"What's it for then?"

"Dynamite. What else? But not for robbing banks. For the revolution."

"The *revolution*? The Irish got one, too?" He was

laughing. The idea struck him as absurd. "It must be catching," he said. "Like the crabs."

Mallory's reaction was a sour grimace. Juan didn't care. If he had learned nothing else in life, he had learned the treachery of revolutionaries. They killed for myths, for illusions, always in the name of some promised paradise, always for their fellow countrymen, never for themselves. Then they turned out the way Madero had, and Huerta after him. Hah. A man who wasn't selfish, who didn't act only for himself, wasn't meant to be trusted.

"The last revolution we had," he said, "it was terrible, like a bullfight where the matador wins but gets knocked on the head and comes out loco, with no brain left. People get crazy in revolutions. Good men like Villa, they become generals. You know Villa was a bandit. With iron balls. You know what happened? When he became general, he decided he didn't like the President. So he became a revolutionary again. For what? So he can become a general again if he wins."

Juan spat in disgust. "What bullshit!" he said. Something occured to him. "Hey, you didn't come here to—?"

Mallory's back was to him as he worked on the motorcycle. His head shook slowly. "No, one was enough for me," he said softly. He stood up and swung his leg over the machine.

"So?" Juan opened his arms as he said it.

"So, goodby." Mallory kicked the starter and the motorcycle came to life. Juan opened his mouth to speak but a sudden roar cut him off. Spraying pebbles, the bike moved off across the rocky terrain. "Hey, wait—" Juan called, but was drowned out as Mallory accelerated.

Impulsively, Juan drew his pistol and fired at the rapidly retreating machine. He shot without aiming, emptying his gun. The motorcycle shuddered, then slithered to a halt. Mallory turned and looked down at his rear tire. It was flat again. Gasoline poured out of the tank and quickly evaporated on the warm, dry ground.

Mallory dismounted, stared for a moment at the gasoline streaming from the tank, then began walking back toward Juan. He put his hands in his overcoat pocket and lowered his head. He seemed pensive.

With his head still down and his lips pursed in thought, Mallory strolled slowly past as if Juan didn't exist. Juan was puzzled. What the hell was he doin?

Too late, it hit him. Mallory was already in the coach when Juan gave a cry and began running toward him. Through the open window he could see the Irishman standing before the small statue of St. Frances. In his hand was—Juan paused. The object looked like a candle. The mad bastard was going to pray!

Juan watched as Mallory lit the candle and placed it next to the statue. Mallory crossed himself and came down from the coach. He mussed the hair of Chulo, who had been standing on the running board looking in, and gently took the boy's hand. The expression on his face was serene, almost unearthly, as he came toward Juan. Juan felt a moment of awe at the purity and power of the man's faith; the Irish must truly be devout. But why the hell pray now?

"Well, what now?" Juan asked.

Mallory's voice was soft and composed when he spoke. "Duck, you sucker!" he said and pulled Chulo to the ground.

A mournful cry escaped Juan before the coach blew. The explosion knocked him off his feet and sent bits of wood screaming past his head. His ears rang in pain. His shoulder throbbed and his head reeled.

He got slowly to his feet and looked at the ruins of his coach. The carriage, blown free of the wheels, was tilted at a precarious angle to the ground. Its insides had been completely destroyed. Nothing but tattered fabric and charred wood remained. Pieces of the shattered stove were strewn about the ground.

In despair, Juan approached the smoking ruins. "My

house," he mumbled, and was surprised at his enormous sense of loss. Crazy, but he had really begun to think of the coach as a house, one on wheels that he could take with him wherever he went.

By the time he remembered the Irishman, Mallory was already busy unstrapping his suitcase from the crippled motorcycle. "Okay," Juan said. "Go work for the German. Okay." His voice sounded tight and hollow.

Mallory flashed him an ironic smile, scooped up his suitcase and turned to leave. He looked back for a moment. "Which way to Lucainena?" he said.

Some buried reservoir of joy burst in Juan. It raced like electricity through his body and rippled into his head, where it told him he had not lost after all. It forced him to smile and it made his voice crackle when he said, "Uh, uh, Firecracker. You gotta find it yourself."

Mallory shrugged and began walking toward the deserted plain. "Mexico is big," Juan called after him. "You'll see. For you it's gonna be very big."

He watched the Irishman's back grow smaller, the overcoat standing out like a thin black pen against the horizon, the bowler like a drop of ink.

"Get the horses," he ordered.

"You gonna kill him now, Papa?" Chulo asked.

"Better than that," Juan said.

Chapter Five

They kept to the side and about three hundred feet behind Mallory. He walked briskly for the first two hours, never acknowledging their presence by looking around. He was heading in the best of directions, toward the dryest part of the desert, and Juan did nothing to detract or deter him.

Mallory walked for four hours after nightfall, not stopping once. An incredibly bright moon, bright as only the desert can make it, lit his way. When he finally stopped, it was in a small gully which gave him shelter from the wind. He lay down abruptly under the lean of the gully wall and went to sleep.

In the morning he rose, brushed the dust from himself and headed on his way. He tramped over the hard, rocky terrain until nearly noon. His pace slowed with the rising heat of the sun. Dust turned his overcoat and bowler gray. He kept switching the suitcase from hand to hand, and by the time he paused to rest, he had already stumbled several times.

Mallory set down the suitcase and for the first time took out his flask. He shook it by his ear, measuring the supply, then unscrewed the top and tilted it toward his mouth. Juan quickly pulled a rifle from its sheath and shot the flask from Mallory's hand.

The Irishman wheeled around angrily. His hand darted under his coat and came partially away with a pistol. He paused. Juan smiled confidently. Mallory was far out of pistol range.

"If you change your mind, Firecracker," Juan yelled, "just call me."

Mallory grabbed his suitcase and turned away.

They rode with him for the rest of the day. In midafternoon, Mallory fell down for the first time; an hour later he was falling every quarter mile. He dragged his feet heavily across the dry ground and paused ever more frequently to rest. Once when he fell, he staggered up facing Juan. Even from a distance Juan could see that the Irishman's face was burned and his lips were swollen. Soft European flesh, he thought. He was pleased.

Only one thing was wrong. In his failing state, Mallory had strayed from a straight course. Instead of trekking into the heart of the desert, he was now bissecting a corner of it, stumbling toward the desert edge. The sun would have to do its job quickly.

By late afternoon Juan could make out the lines of a building a mile or two ahead. Mallory was heading for it. The lines sharpened as they neared. The building was an old shack, crumbling, with the walls half-caved in. Wild grass grew lushly around it. There would be water there.

Mallory broke into a lurching run as he approached the shack. Cursing silently, Juan kicked his horse and closed the gap between them. Mallory burst through the grass. Behind it, to the side of the shack, lay an abandoned vegetable garden. A half-dozen watermelons, heavy and green, grew untended there. In a final burst, Mallory reeled toward them. He bent to pick up a melon. Juan took quick aim and shot it away. Mallory reached for a piece of the shattered fruit, but another shot warned him off. Methodically, Juan destroyed the remaining melons.

Mallory never noticed the small pond to the lee of the shack. He teetered blindly out of the garden in a line that took him away from the desert and the shack. Somehow, he managed to cover another two miles.

It ended at a muddy puddle which lay at the bottom of a steep incline. Chulo, Napolean, Sebastian, and Nene stood on the crest high above the puddle, which was only a few feet around, and peed down into it just as Mallory began to drink. The Irishman raised half-closed eyes to them. His lips moved in a silent curse. Then he fainted.

They lifted Mallory gently in the air and layed him across a horse. They threw a poncho over him and led the horse away.

The crumbling walls of a fort loomed up before them after they had ridden a few miles. The fort's towers thrust proudly in the air, but no sentry could be seen in them. The iron gates were twisted, useless masses blown open once and never set back on their swingpins.

Inside, weeds grew in ragged clumps around the courtyard. A low, stone building dominated the yard. Its paint was peeling and its wooden portico rotted in the sun.

They made a place for Mallory inside the building, spreading a serape on the dirty floor. More weeds sprouted through the cracks in the planking.

"Watch him carefully," Juan ordered before he rode away. "Don't leave him."

He left the fort feeling a sense of accomplishment. Only one thing remained to do and Mallory would be his.

The *niños* disobeyed Juan as soon as he was out of sight. They left Mallory with their grandfather and went scavenging through the abandoned buildings of the fort. Juan's men, meanwhile, tended the horses.

Nino cleared the hearth and lighted a fire. From a pouch he carried with him, he took out some *tostadas* and baked it over the fire. He ate slowly, listening to the low breathing of the Irishman and wishing for some tequila. Fefe drifted in to tell him he had found the messhall kitchen. They would all be over there for a while, he said, cooking some *atole,* a thick maize gruel, so be sure to guard the Irishman closely.

Nino nodded. Okay. A half hour later he was alseep.

Mallory awoke after Juan had been gone for several hours. He squinted in the flickering light from the fire-place at what appeared to be faces overhead. His eyes took focus. Nene and Benito peered down at him from the ceiling's disconnected beams. Each was crouched on a beam; apparently they had been playing up there for some time.

Mallory raised himself on one elbow and looked around. The old man was sitting against a wall in the corner, sleeping with his head on his chest. Sebastian's face appeared briefly in the window, then vanished. Mallory rolled over and sat up. Pepe smiled at him from his hiding place in a cleft in the wall and stuck out his tongue.

The sound of approaching horses drifted into the room. A moment later Juan's voice echoed softly against the stone walls. "Hey, Irish. Hey, *niños*. It's me."

Nene and Benito dropped from the ceiling and ran toward the door. Pepe shook the old man awake and then dashed after his brothers. Nino followed in a daze.

Alone, Mallory struggled to his feet and staggered across the room. He was still very weak, but the need for haste drove him on. He fumbled with his suitcase, got it open and reached inside for several sticks of dynamite. As quickly as his trembling fingers permitted, he attached fuse wire to the dynamite and wedged it into a corner of the room.

Mallory refastened the suitcase, took hold of it and began backing out of the room, paying out wire as he went. He moved directly away from the door toward a breach in the opposite wall. He backed through the breach.

The night enveloped him. The air from the desert was harsh and the stars sparked dizzily overhead. His head spun off into some hot, dark tomb. He shook it violently to clear it. Still unsteady, he managed to retreat until his back touched a low wall some thirty feet from the building.

From the suitcase he took out a small detonator. He set the wooden box on the ground and attached the fuse wire.

On the other side of the fort Juan was calling his name. Mallory held his breath and waited. Through the gap in the building wall he could make out the vague outlines of the doorway. Soon that bastard would come through the door. His hand tightened on the detonator handle.

The voices stopped. He could hear the crickets but not Juan's gutteral rumble or the chattering of the boys. Mallory peered through a haze into the building. Nothing. Long moments crawled by. Still nothing. Mallory rose from his kneeling position beside the detonator and lurched a half-dozen steps closer to the building. In the dim light, he could just make out the indistinct silhouettes of four men standing in the entrance.

He wheeled to go back for the detonator. A voice cut him off.

"Hey, Irish, what are you doing out here?"

He felt dizzy. He stood helplessly watching Juan's bulk emerge out of the darkness. Several other shadowy figures were behind him. His sons. His men.

His men?

"Who's in the building?" Mallory blurted. "Who are they?"

"Well . . ." Juan said laconically, "it's a long story."

They were all around him now. In the corner of his vision he saw a small shadowy figure move toward the detonator, then pause. Mallory checked an impulse to race for the box. Maybe the *niños* wouldn't notice it. He started to say something to Juan. The shock of awareness stopped him. Terrified, he spun violently around. Yes, the shadow had moved again and now held the small box in his hand. He recognized Chulo even as he screamed.

"NO. NO, DON'T."

Too late. The boy had already begun to depress the plunger.

The blinding glare hit them a fraction before the sound. Mallory felt the ground tremble beneath his feet. The concussion hurled him backward.

He struggled to stay erect. A chunk of stone debris struck his leg, and he screamed from the sharp pain.

Juan was down on his rump wearing an astonished look when the dust subsided. Exhausted and in shock, Mallory lowered himself to the ground beside him. He held his head in his hands for several minutes and allowed the nausea to pass. "All right," he said wearily when he finally looked up. "Who were they?"

Little Chulo answered excitedly. "Aschenbach, one captain, two soldiers. All blown to hell."

Aghast, Mallory felt a dank chill sweep over him. He stared at Juan in mute horror. Juan smiled back at him.

"Fantastic, eh, Firecracker?" Juan said. "No more contract with the German to worry about. You're free now." He snickered. "I'll even let you drink now." He opened a flask and offered it to Mallory, who didn't move.

"I tell you," Juan bubbled on. "It was very hard to convince them to come." He thrust the flask at Mallory again. "Here, go drink. Go on, drink." Mallory took the flask and put it to his mouth.

"Aschenbach, he couldn't believe you sent me to get him. Ha. But when I said you found a big silver vein here, that greedy bastard came running."

Mallory stopped gulping water. It took all his energy to speak. "The soldiers. Why the soldiers?" he gasped. He felt drained.

"Oh, you gotta understand our country. Huerta stole the silver mines when he became President and cut the pay of the miners. So they refused to work. Okay? Huerta sends in his soldiers and shoots a few miners. They go back to work. Then Huerta hires Aschenbach to run the mines. Aschenbach cuts the pay even more and puts the savings in his pocket. Aschenbach is also stealing silver on the side. How does he get away with it? He pays off the army captain. They were in cahoots."

Mallory shook his head in disbelief. Could Juan be inventing this? No, not from what he'd heard of Huerta.

"That captain." Juan was still gushing. "He almost screwed everything up. At the last minute he said, 'You bring the Irishman to us.' Then when I tell them a dynamite stick blew up in your hand, they moved their asses to get here before you died." Juan roared. " I never did so much talking in my life."

"I don't understand. Why did you want Aschenbach to come here? What good would it have done?"

"Oh, I figured I'd hold him hostage for a while and maybe threaten to kill him until you agreed to go with me. That way you couldn't go to work for him. Now I don't have a hostage. I got something better."

"Oh, yeah? What's that?"

"Ah, *amigo*. You got three dead soldiers from your dynamite. Very serious. You're gonna have to explain it. And what if they don't believe you? You know the army, they get very nervous if you blow up a captain."

Juan put a consoling arm around Mallory's shoulder. "What you gonna do now, huh? The only one you got to help you is your friend Juan."

"Listen, you fucken chicken thief," Mallory snapped. "I don't need your help to know when I've been screwed."

He didn't say anything else for a long moment. He suddenly felt very tired, defeated. "All right," he sighed. "What do you want me to do?"

Juan leaped to his feet. His face was aglow. "Let's go to Mesa Verde," he cried.

Chapter Six

"Hey, Irish, we will be rich."

They were following along a railroad track. A vast flat plain that seemed continuous with the sky stretched out before them. The sun was high overhead.

Juan rode down the middle of the track. Mallory rode sullenly to his right, a stark figure in the black coat and bowler against the high blue sky.

"Tell me something," he said. "Is the bank the only thing you remember about Mesa Verde?"

"Uh, uh. I remember a place you eat. A very special place. Like no place else. You go inside, sit down, and right before your eyes . . ." Juan spread his hands open like an actor welcoming applause.

"Right before your eyes you see the bank," Mallory finished the sentence.

Juan laughed. The low clatter of an approaching train mingled with his laughter. He ignored the sound. "And you know what? Mesa Verde is only the start. We'll be famous." His hand swept the air as if painting a sign. "Juan and John, specialists in banks."

The train whistled.

"No, no," Juan rumbled on. He was enjoying the game. "I got it: 'Johnny and Johnny!' Sounds better, more American." He beamed at Mallory. "We're gonna go to America, Firecracker. They got cities with nothing but banks—Colorado, California, Texas, Austria."

Mallory guffawed. The train whistled again, very close.

"Think of the future ahead of us!!"

"I'm thinking of the train behind you," Mallory said calmly.

"Jesus Christ!"

Juan kicked his horse and whipped the reins hard to the left. The horse sprang free of the tracks with only a moment to spare. With a roar, the train hurtled past.

It separated Juan from Mallory. Juan looked around him frantically. His entire gang was on his side of the tracks. That meant Mallory was alone on the other side. "Shit," he screamed.

He jumped to the ground and bent over to look under the moving train. Through the wheels he could see the legs of Mallory's horse.

He tried to gauge the train's speed. It was moving fast—but was it moving fast enough? He imagined making the leap himself. It would be difficult. But not, he realized with a sinking feeling, impossible.

He cursed God, St. Christopher, the Pope. He compared Mallory to a pig, to a whore, to a pus-running sore. He ranted that the Irish were scum and their mothers bearers of social diseases.

None of it helped. Mallory was gone when the train passed.

There was only one thing to do.

Nine hours later Juan and his brood boarded the train at Cuzco. Several soldiers were slumped around the station. The troops ignored them while they waited on the platform until a peacock captain came around and ordered his men to be alert. At that, a boyish private shuffled over to Juan and asked, "See any revolutionaries?"

"No, *amigo.*"

"Bandits?"

Juan pointed to his two youngest. "Those two. Very dangerous. Be careful when you arrest them."

The soldier laughed and shambled away.

The train was nearly empty. Juan slumped next to a window and stretched out his legs. He glanced out but saw only his reflection in the night. With his hat over his eyes, he went to sleep.

He awoke when the train pulled into Aguadiz. The door at the end of the car opened and a tall, lean, middle-aged man came in. He was wearing a neat brown suit and the shirt under it looked newly cleaned. His hand held a black leather doctor's bag.

The man strolled toward them, indifferent to the hostile glances from the boys. With silent authority, he motioned to Juan's sons to clear a space for him. Under his glasses, his eyes were deep-set and intelligent.

With obvious resentment, the boys obeyed. The man settled into the seat facing Juan and took a book from his bag. He opened it and began to read. The title was *Surgical Pathology*.

They rode in silence for a long while. Once when Chulo and Nene began to squeal, the doctor cut them off with a harsh glance. Juan regarded the man with amusement. Even old man Nino and Fefe, who considered himself such a tough hombre, seemed cowed. Yet the man hadn't said a word.

A sudden loud screeching of the brakes suddenly ended Juan's musings. He hurtled forward but managed to brake himself on the window sill. The train jolted to a stop and stood hissing softly.

Juan wiped the window and peered out curiously. Nothing. The sound of a handle rattling made him look toward the end of the car. The door slammed open and a man in a dark uniform climbed aboard. A policeman!! The cut of his jacket marked him as a member of Huerta's "elite" squad—loyal, tough, ruthless, and trained in torture.

Juan exchanged glances with the doctor, then pulled stiffly back in his seat. He tensed as the cop came down the aisle. The doctor's hard face screwed up in puzzlement as he looked at Juan. Juan's breath caught. A clammy hand gripped his spine. Still wearing the curious expression, the cop passed him and walked down through the car.

Juan's eyes followed him. The cop reached the connecting doorway, then stopped as if struck by a sudden thought and wheeled around. Juan darted low in his seat and pulled his sombrero over his face.

He could hear the cop's returning footsteps. His teeth clenched and he shrank in upon himself. The footsteps stopped and a hand raised his hat. Juan smiled up.

"This isn't the first time I've seen you," the cop said. His hair gave off the odor of pomade.

"No?" Juan said meekly.

The cop brought his face closer. His eyes narrowed and his mouth set in a grim line. "No, it's not the first time."

"But it's the last—" With enormous force, Juan suddenly flung himself forward. His hand plunged toward the cop's stomach. A knife slid with a faint sucking sound into flesh, and the cop collapsed with a shudder into Juan's arms.

Juan twisted him quickly around and half carried him to the door. He worked the door open and pushed the cop off the speeding train.

He turned and walked back toward the doctor. The knife was still in his hand.

"Hey!"

Another cop was standing at the end of the car. He sighted down along a pistol aimed at Juan's head. The door to the next car stood open behind him.

"Drop that knife, you bastard," the cop said.

Juan let the knife slide to the ground. Slowly, he raised his hands. The cop came down the car toward him. Juan held his breath.

The cop stopped. "I can't miss from this distance," he warned.

What happened next stunned Juan. The cop never got a

chance to say or do anything else. A hand came toward him and pressed a derringer against his ribs. He looked down at the small gun and straightened in alarm. His fingers opened and the pistol dropped to the floor.

Juan had expected help from one of his people. Instead, to his amazement, the doctor was leaning forward in his seat with the derringer. Unbelievable.

With a leap Juan fell on the frightened cop. He grabbed the man around the neck with one arm and dragged him to the door. The cop whimpered when he saw what was about to happen, and he cried out in terror as Juan effortlessly threw him from the moving train. For a moment Juan regretted having let him live. Such screaming.

The doctor was absorbed again in his book when Juan returned to his seat. His face was composed and impassive, refusing even to acknowledge Juan's existence, or the stares of the *niños*. Strange man, Juan thought. Maybe he just hates police. He sat down and pulled his hat over his eyes, wondering with wary concern what kind of doctor carries a gun.

The thought pecked at him all the way to Mesa Verde. He dozed fitfully, amid the din of bickering and laughter from his boys, and whenever he looked up there was the doctor, as intent on his medical text as if he were reading a novel in a soft chair beside a fireplace. A curious case himself.

He learned nothing else about the man. At Mesa Verde, the doctor rose and left the train as coolly as he had entered, while Juan's kids still had their faces glued to the windows. They were babbling in excitement and pointing to a peeling station sign which announced their destination.

The platform was deserted save for a column of soldiers guarding several shabbily dressed men. Juan ignored the sight and shepherded his sons away from the soldiers.

"Mesa Verde, *muchachos*," he announced, feeling and sounding lyrical.

The boys looked at him in dismay. He turned to Nino. "Mesa Verde, *papacito*," he said, and settled for a wan smile.

"Hey, Papa." Chulo tugged on his arm. "Are those men bandits?" He pointed at the prisoners.

"No. They're revolutionaries. They're not smart enough to be bandits."

"Revolutionaries don't make no money, huh?"

"They only make trouble," Juan said.

He looked toward the prisoners just in time to see one of them shove a guard aside and race toward him. He ducked instinctively and tried to push his sons from the prisoner's path. Almost simultaneously several guns crashed. The impact of the bullets hurled the prisoner down onto his face almost at Juan's feet.

He herded his sons quickly away from the corpse and off the platform, before they became conspicuous. Motherofjesus, he wondered, what's going on here?

Mesa Verde shocked him. Except for soldiers, the streets were deserted. Platoons marched on every other street, some heading in the direction of the train station, others obviously on patrol.

The walls of nearly every building they passed were either scarred by fire or pockmarked with bullet holes. Several houses stood half demolished, the tiles from their roofs scattered in the streets. Mesa Verde looked like a city under siege.

Two of Juan's men, Pancho and Amando, broke their usual silences to complain. Both seemed as much in distress as Juan felt.

"It must be the rebels are fighting here," Pancho said. "Maybe we should leave."

Juan didn't answer. They kept walking. Everywhere, walls were papered with the same poster: an elegantly clad grandfatherly looking man offering bread to a family of peons. "The Governor loves his people!" the poster claimed.

They turned a corner and came into a square with a blast-shattered fountain. At one end, near a wall, a cluster of soldiers stood with three men whose hands were tied behind their backs. Two were obviously peons; the third, a man in a business suit with a dignified moustache, looked like a banker. Near them a man in a blue poncho was busily painting white stripes on a wall.

Juan and his brood stopped and watched the man paint the last of three horizontal stripes. From across the square the soldiers eyed them suspiciously. When the painter finished, the soldiers shoved their prisoners against the striped wall. At the command of an officer, the troops then took up firing positions a dozen paces away.

The officer's voice drifted faintly across the clearing. "Do you have a last wish?" he asked the three men. There was no answer. Then one of the peons turned toward a poster on the wall and spit in the smiling face of the governor.

Angered, the officer barked a command to fire. The shots flung the prisoners back against the wall as if they were rag dolls. Their bodies jiggled in a lunatic dance. They were dead before they hit the ground.

Confused and despairing, Juan led the others away from the square and through the ruins of a house destroyed by cannon fire. In a corner, half buried under the rubble, were the tattered remnants of a child's doll. Madness, he thought. He had no dynamite. The city was crawling with soldiers. The rebels were presumably somewhere close by making the soldiers tense and suspicious. The civilians were too cowed to come out in the streets, so there was no hope for them to panic and create confusion. How could he possibly rob the bank? If there was one left.

"Hey," he said to Nino. "You sure this is Mesa Verde?"

The old man merely shrugged.

A cavalry platoon rode by in a cloud of dust. They

crossed the street when it passed and turned another corner. Nino stopped. He nodded mutely toward a building in front of him. Juan froze and stared trancelike at the building. The sight was like walking into a brick wall.

The building was massive and old. The walls were cracked and the portico was slanted at an angle, as if one of its supporting columns had shrunken upon itself. In the design of the columns, in the ponderous friezes along the roof line, in the elaborate grillwork of its windows, the building was unapologetically pretentious. The sign over the portico read: BANCO NACIONAL DE MESA VERDE.

Two armed sentinels stood near the carved doorway looking suspiciously at Juan and his troop. Suddenly aware that he was becoming obvious, Juan smiled and, beckoning the others to follow, strolled casually across the street. He spotted a tavern and headed for it.

Something brought him up short. God, was it? Through the tavern window he could see the back of a lean figure wearing a bowler hat. The man tilted his head back and brought a flask upward. As he did, he turned his head slightly.

Mallory!

Chapter Seven

"Get out of here! I gotta take care of something."

Nino and the boys moved reluctantly away, casting troubled looks back at Juan. He ignored them and marched toward the tavern.

He entered softly as a cat. Mallory was alone at a table, his back to the door. The black overcoat was not in sight; he was wearing a plain gray suit now. There was no suitcase, either.

The tavern was nearly empty. Two peons talked quietly at a table in the corner of the room. The proprietor could be seen working in a kitchen at the rear.

Juan crept silently up behind Mallory. With every step, he felt the bile rise in him. He stopped just behind the Irishman, who seemed intent on ladling chili onto his plate. Slowly, Juan eased his pistol from its holster.

"With beans or without?"

What? Was Mallory talking to himself?

"You want your chili with beans or without?" Mallory repeated, louder now. He barely turned his head.

"Huh?"

"You going to eat standing up?" Mallory spooned a mouthful of chili.

Incredulous, Juan numbly lowered himself into the chair across from Mallory. Mallory pushed a plate in front of him and continued eating from the pan. With a shrug, Juan picked up a spoon and reluctantly mouthed some chili.

His gaze remained riveted on the Irishman. Somehow he had to set matters right.

"Listen, Firecracker. You try to get away again and I'm gonna shoot you. You understand?" His voice was flat.

Mallory chewed impassively. "Who's trying to get away," he said thickly. "A train comes along. I was on the right side, so I took it." He looked up. "Besides, I knew you'd come to Mesa Verde."

"Mesa Verde! Shit, what a city! What the hell's going on here? There's more soldiers than flies."

"Good. Right?"

"Good?"

"Sure, where there's revolution, there's confusion. And where there's confusion, a guy who knows what he wants stands a good chance of getting it." Mallory scraped the pan and stuffed the last of the chili in his mouth.

Juan started to reply but was waved silent. The two peons who had been sitting in the corner passed their table. Mallory's eyes followed them out.

Juan suddenly was aware of someone standing behind him. He turned. The proprietor, a giant of a man, was studying him from about a foot away. He stepped to the side of the table.

"This him?" he said.

Mallory nodded. Juan stiffened and warily moved his hand toward his pistol.

"Okay, follow me." The proprietor walked away.

"I'm 'him' who?" Juan whispered hoarsely.

Mallory watched the proprietor until he was out of earshot, then leaned across the table and whispered back, "You trust me?"

Juan shook his head emphatically. Trust Mallory? His nitroglycerin near a hot fire was more reliable.

The Irishman sighed. He pointed out the window. The bank was clearly visible through it. "You want to get inside there, don't you?" he said.

Juan grinned.

"Well, I'm going to give you the chance."

Mallory got up and followed the proprietor into the back room.

Juan hung back, suspicious. Mallory was too cool and too clever to be followed blindly. To trust him was like trusting the President. He might act in your favor, but the odds were about the same as the odds against getting the pimple disease from a whore; the only way to avoid it was not get in bed with the girl in the first place. Besides, he had learned that survival always depended on commanding the situation, never being commanded. But not to follow now . . . ? That would mean no explosives, no bank, no money.

Juan hurried after Mallory.

The Irishman and the proprietor were waiting for him in the back room. The smell of onions hung heavily in the air. They went through a narrow doorway and down a steep staircase to a dim cellar. Wine barrels and shelves stacked with bottles surrounded them.

The proprietor approached a tall wine rack set against the back wall, gripped the frame and pulled hard toward him. With a faint sigh, the shelf swung outward to reveal a door.

The big man knocked. A moment later the door opened slowly and Mallory motioned Juan to follow him. Warily, Juan obeyed.

They came into a small, musty, windowless room. The smell of dust and sweat stung Juan. An oil lamp set up in one corner cast a weak, flickering light across several dark figures and created an eerie, sepulchral mood.

Juan saw in mid-room the naked back of a man stripped to the waist. On either side, a peon held tightly to an arm, pinioning the man between them. Seven or eight other men scattered around the room were looking on indifferently.

The flash of a knife caught Juan's eye. A tall, lean figure was standing before the bare-chested man testing the edge of the blade. Juan recognized the figure: the doctor from the train.

The realization stunned him. He turned to Mallory, who only signaled him to keep quiet. Incredible! What was the doctor doing here? What was he about to witness? Torture?

The doctor approached the man and studied his chest. He brought the knife up, and the man recoiled instinctively.

"Don't move, goddamit!" the doctor snapped. And to the others, "Hold him still."

A cry of pain shattered the stillness. Juan flinched. A violent shudder wracked the bare-chested man and he went limp.

The doctor picked up a cloth and dark bottle. "Relax now," he said softly. He poured some of the bottle's contents down the man's chest, gently patted him with the cloth, then taped a bandage in place. Finished, he looked up and grinned. "If you'd let the infection go any longer, your widow would be paying my bill," he said.

The patient was helped on with his shirt while the doctor packed his equipment into his bag. A heavy, unshaven man wearing a railroad worker's jacket motioned Mallory and Juan forward.

The doctor closed his bag and glanced up. A smile of recognition crossed his face.

"Ah, Mallory," he said.

"Hello, Villega."

Villega nodded. He reached into his pocket and brought out a newspaper clipping, which he waved in the air. "You've hardly joined us at Mesa Verde, and already you're in the papers." He tapped the clipping. "Irish dynamiter wanted for murder," he read.

"You've caused quite a stir, young man. Killing the captain, that's nothing. But the German? Not even Pancho Villa has dared to take on a foreign capitalist."

So, Juan thought, they found the bodies and someone

remembered it was Mallory who supposedly sent for Aschenbach. Juan looked at him. The Irishman's mouth was clenched and his jaw muscles were bulging. His face had gone gaunt and hard, like a man confronting his jailer for the first time.

"It seems that even his Majesty's secret service would like to get their hands on you." Villega was toying with him now. "Well, my friend, I think we'll keep you for a while. You're a real asset to us—even if you do drink too much."

Mallory's reply was curious. "Who says I drink too much?" he snapped. Funny man, Juan mused, not even interested in how he might be an asset to Villega. Or perhaps just not showing it.

With professional dexterity, Villega jabbed a stiff finger at Mallory's stomach, causing him to grimace. "Your liver does," he said. "It changes your coloring."

The railroad worker pointed at Juan. "What about this one?" he asked Villega.

"He's all right. Except that when he's operating, he makes deeper incisions than I do."

"Well, without no training my hand's kind of heavy. . . ."

Mallory was staring at him, clearly surprised. For a moment, Juan savored the Irishman's bewilderment.

"We did a little job together," he finally explained. "Me and the doctor."

Villega nodded in agreement. Smiling, he rummaged through his bag and took out a thermometer case. "And now we've got another job," he said.

He opened the case to reveal a thin, folded sheet of paper, which he spread on a table. Juan saw a map of a city sketched on the paper. Mesa Verde, he guessed.

Villega waved for silence. "I have good news." His eyes were glowing. "In two days Villa and Zapata will attack simultaneously from north and south. We here, like those in other cities, must begin parallel actions of harassment.

Right now, any spark could light the fire. Huerta's downfall is only a question of weeks."

A low rumble of pleasure swept the room. In a corner a
pale, thin man began coughing violently. A cigarette was
squeezed between his bloodless lips.

Villega looked at him. "Whereas Miguel's downfall is
only a question of hours if he doesn't stop smoking."

Laughter rippled through the room.

Juan was silent and pensive. Now he understood: *These*
were the revolutionaries. His mouth tasted sour. He
studied the others. They were staring raptly at Villega,
aglow with the sense of impending action. Each of
them clearly was prepared to die, Juan realized with disgust. And for what? Would the next President be any
better? Was Huerta better than Madero had been? Would
the laws be any different? The rich would still own all the
land and the *nobles* would still sip Spanish wine in their
elegant haciendas and pretend to be descendents of Napo-
leon and the Church would still tell the peons that life was
as it was because God had so willed it.

"The committee has made a few minor changes in the
plans," Villega was saying.

Juan thought of Zapata and Villa. Zapata, that mad
Indian from the South. He and his tenant farmers and
their crazy idea to give the land back to the Indians. Hah.
The Indians hadn't owned the land for four hundred
years.

And who had they rebelled against first? Madero! That
weak old man who at least wanted to give them the land
when he was President even if he didn't have the balls to
do it. Now that Huerta had murdered Madero and become President himself, did Zapata think he could defeat
Huerta? If he couldn't beat Madero, how could he beat
someone like Huerta. And if he did, so what? The next
President would be the same. No politician in Mexico
would give the land back to the Indians.

Villega was pointing at the map. "We'll attack in four

places at one time. Redondo and his men will take care of the guardhouse and the old prison. . . ."

And Villa. A clown! Sure, he had been a good bandit. His men worshipped him. He was daring and clever. But what happened? He decided to play soldier. To play general. It didn't matter who he was fighting, just as long as he was fighting. Who was it against the first time? Oh, yes, Diaz. Three years ago when Diaz was still President. Sure. Villa fought to make Madero President instead of Diaz. And who did he serve under? Huerta! And now he was fighting against Huerta, against his own general. And for still another man, Carranza. And if Carranza became President, you could bet Villa would find some reason to fight him.

Juan stared blankly at the map as Villega pointed to various buildings and droned on. "Those with Ruiz and Antonio will take on the regulars' barracks. Francisco and his men at the railroad depot. Ortega, the post office. Once the enemy is busy on four fronts, we'll move against our real objective."

Absently, Juan wondered what was the real objective, then dismissed the thought. Who cared?

"Are you still agreed?" Villega looked at Mallory, who nodded. "Do you need men?"

"I only need one."

Villega gestured toward Juan. "Him?"

"Him who?!" Juan exploded. "Me? To do what?"

"Attack the bank," Mallory said.

The words jarred him. He opened his mouth but no sound came out. Finally, he managed to breathe, "That's right, me and him. Mallory and me. . . ."

For some reason, the others were staring at him with undisguised admiration.

"Don't worry," Juan gushed. "We'll take care of everything. Everything. We got our own men, our own dynamite, pistols, ammo, everything. You do the rest and leave the bank to Juan and John. Johnny and Johnny."

"Good," Villega said crisply. "I hope you make it."

"Me, too."

Villega pulled a watch from his pocket. "We'll meet again tonight to discuss details. I'll have to go now. I left a woman in labor—and she can't wait until the revolution is over."

Villega extended his hand. One by one, the other men approached and grimly stacked their hands atop his. Mallory motioned to Juan to do the same.

"Land and Liberty!" Villega shouted.

Motherofjesus, Juan thought, a doctor echoing the slogan of a landless farmer, Zapata. Stupidity.

"Land and Liberty!" the others cried. Juan mumbled along with them.

He watched Villega retrieve his bag and head for the door with the others following. He was aware that he was grinning stupidly as he edged over to Mallory.

"Don't tell me nothing," he whispered. "They move in and we remove." He laughed softly. "Land and Liberty? How about Gold and Money instead." He nodded to the rebels. "What assholes!"

Beside him, Mallory was also laughing softly.

Chapter Eight

The sky was deep blue and beautiful. Two soldiers stood lazily in the shade of the portico, guarding the entrance to the bank. The few people who passed all seemed in a hurry.

Juan watched intently from across the street, crouched with his boys, his father, and his men behind the windows and the door of the tavern. His eyes combed every corner, alert for every movement, for signs that something might be amiss. Nothing appeared to be. A keen sensation washed over him, sharpening his senses. Anticipation. He could almost smell the money.

Behind him the tavern was empty. Only Mallory remained, seated coolly at a table in the rear, staring at the door. He was wearing his black overcoat and bowler again, and the suitcase was by his side. Juan ignored him. Irish's job was mostly done; the crucial part was now up to him and his boys. He looked them over quickly. Each was clenching a rifle and seemed intent on the bank. He smiled. They were experienced. They would do well.

Mallory took out a pocket watch, looked at it and signaled to Pepe standing in the kitchen doorway. Pepe relayed the signal to Napolean, who rose before one of the windows and flashed the sign to little Chulo.

Chulo was across the street, round the corner of the bank. Juan watched proudly as the boy came to attention and started on his mission. Even from the distance it was clear that Chulo's face had been scrubbed and his hair combed back like a choir boy's. He looked the picture of innocence as he ambled toward the front of the bank pulling a toy wooden train behind him. He was even imitating the sound of a locomotive whistle as he approached.

The guards ignored him.

The boy strolled directly in front of the bank entrance and stopped. A guard looked at him and barked. "Get out of the way. You're blocking the door."

The clatter of heavy rifle fire in the distance suddenly rent the air. Juan saw the two guards look confusedly at each other and step out into the street, seeking the source of the shots. One of them pointed in the direction of the guardhouse. They both brought their rifles up, ready to fire.

Behind them, unobserved, Chulo edged along the entrance door with his train. He passed one of the massive columns flanking the door and kept walking. The train went no farther.

Juan watched the string with which Chulo had pulled the toy grow longer as the boy came out from under the portico and into the street. A few passersby were running for cover now as the distant shooting grew more intense. None of them noticed Chulo, nor did the guards.

He broke into a run and raced for the tavern. The string unwound from a spool beneath his shirt as he came on. He avoided the main door and disappeared into an alley at the side of the building.

Across the street now Juan saw two officers come out of the bank. Their uniforms were starched and new. Some soldiers trailed behind them.

"What the hell's happening?" one of them bellowed.

A guard turned toward him. "Must be a rebel attack, Captain," he said.

Chulo dashed into the tavern dining room from the kitchen door at the rear. Juan winked at him; he had

indeed done well. The boy ran to Mallory and handed
him the string.

Quickly and deftly, Mallory split the end into two
strands. He reached under the table and brought up a
small detonating box. To this he attached the two ends of
the string.

Outside, more soldiers were running out of the bank.
The officers were hoarsely shouting orders to the men,
positioning them in front of the building.

"Look at all the troops," Juan whispered to nobody in
particular. "Must be a helluva lot of money in there." He
looked at Mallory, who waved him over to the table.

"You know how to work this?" Mallory handed him a
bundle of dynamite sticks tied together.

"Fast fuse?"

"No, normal rate. Thirty seconds."

Juan nodded and carefully eased the dynamite under
his shirt. Mallory checked his watch, gestured for the
others to get down, and crouched under the table himself.
His hand smacked against the detonator handle.

The explosion shattered the tavern windows and blew
off the doors. Dust flew into the room. Juan heard debris
hammering against the tavern walls and felt a hot blast
and a roaring in his ears.

He looked up and squinted through the settling dust
out the window. The entire front of the bank where the
toy train had sat was smashed and in ruins, and a gaping
hole yawned where the carved doors had been. The bodies
of soldiers lay scattered under the portico and in the
street.

With a cry, Juan seized two pistols and charged through
the demolished tavern doorway. The *niños* and his men
followed, screaming. Nino brought up the rear.

Fighting could still be heard in the distance but the
street was strangely still. No one rose to resist them as
they raced toward the bank. No one was in sight as they

pounded under the portico, jumped over bodies, and hurtled through the hole where the bank door had been.

Smoke and dust whirled in the air. Juan waited until his eyes adjusted, then began to poke madly around the bank chamber. He kicked aside broken furniture and smashed through a thin, twisted teller's gate. Scorched paper fluttered about in the cage, none of it money.

"The safe," he cried. "Where's the safe?"

He thrashed through some more furniture. Nothing. Coughing dust, he cursed Mallory, the soldiers, his gang. Where the hell was it?

"Hey, Juan. Over here."

One of his men, Pancho, was pointing to an arch over a descending flight of stairs. Over the arch was a faded sign, "SAFE DEPOSIT BOXES," with an arrow pointing down the stairs. "In the basement. Must be down there," Pancho said, and broke for the stairs.

Juan saw him disappear under the arch and take the first few steps with a leap. "Pancho!" he screamed. "Pancho!" Too late. A volley of rifle fire crashed below.

"Pancho!"

Enraged, he grabbed a heavy revolving chair standing nearby. The chair was on wheels. With sudden fury, he sent it rolling across the floor, under the arch, and down the stairs. He raced wildly after it, but pulled up at the top step, sheltered by a wall.

The chair sailed through space and a few shots rang out fitfully, followed by screams. Juan glanced down the stairs and saw the heavy seat crash into four or five soldiers at the bottom. Three of them toppled to the ground, groaned and tried to stand. Juan shot them before they were erect.

The other two looked at him in terror and fled down a corridor. Juan flung himself down the stairs and leaped over the bodies. The two soldiers had just reached the end of the corridor. He managed to kill one of them; the other disappeared around a corner.

The corridor, he noticed now, was lined with doors.

From each hung a heavy chain lock. The sight stabbed him with pleasure. Where there were locks, there must be worth something worth locking up. Oh, Christ, the money must be here.

In an exalted fervor, he lunged toward the nearest door. With a single shot he blew away the chain. Then he kicked outward, smashing the door open, expecting to see the black steel door of a safe loom before him.

There was something else, instead.

Juan gaped in awe at the scene before him. Twenty, twenty-five thin husks of men stared at him. They were all in emaciated rags. Some of them looked sick; others beaten and bruised. Their expressions mingled fear with hope.

Infuriated, he wheeled and rushed toward another door. Who were those men? He didn't care. All that mattered was the money.

He shot away the chain on another door and flung it open. More men. Another scene of misery. Rage convulsed him. The prisoners in the room recoiled at the look on his face.

"Where is it, goddamnit?" he screamed. "Where?"

Pained, frightened faces stared back at him, uncomprehending.

He headed for a third door. Behind him, his men and his sons were caught among the pitiful creatures pouring in bewilderment from the rooms. He heard cries of curiosity and alarm and querulous, confused voices. He ignored them all. The safe had to be somewhere.

The third door only produced more hapless, shabby prisoners. And the fourth and fifth—and the last—the same. By the time he stepped from the last room, blinded by anger and frustration, a throng of uncertain, apprehensive men filled the corridor. He looked at them blankly for a moment, then raced frantically for the end of the corridor and turned the corner. If the safe wasn't here, it must be elsewhere. It must be somewhere. He wouldn't leave the bank till he found it.

He ran down another corridor but stopped abruptly at the sound of approaching steps. Four soldiers emerged from an adjacent passageway. At the sight of him, they brought up their guns. He shot rapidly. To his surprise, the pistol reports were drowned out by the thunder of a rifle fusillage behind him. The four soldiers came bloodily apart and fell in a heap.

Behind him? He spun around. The prisoners were packed into the corridor, following. The first few held rifles, retrieved he guessed from the troops he had killed earlier. Their faces were flushed with excitement, their eyes glowed. They seemed like crazed bulls ready to burst out of a tight corral. He screamed at them to go away, but they misunderstood and yelled back at him.

Motherofjesus! He wheeled and plunged down the corridor. He ran headlong past the passageway from which the soldiers had come, then with a cry twisted about and bolted back toward it. The corner of his eyes had picked up the glint of polished metal. Could it be?

It was! There at the end of the passageway, no more than fifteen feet away, was a gleaming metallic door fashioned with a series of locks and chains. The safe! The safe! It had to be. Delirium burned in him, and he burst in a fever toward the door. His hands ran excitedly over it, testing locks, pulling chains, almost caressing. He felt like a kid.

"Ah, my baby," he mumbled. "This is it."

The sounds of sporadic fighting and of doors being broken open wafted up from behind. He heard the sounds but they made no impression. Only one thing mattered now. Blasting that door open.

He reached frantically under his shirt and brought out the dynamite. He wedged it against one of the door hinges and fumbled for a match. With trembling fingers he lighted the fuse, then dove back around the corner and covered his ears.

The blast was deafening, like a lightning crack against

his head. A dense cloud of smoke exploded from the passageway, blinding him. Ears ringing, eyes burning, he rose and flung himself into the thick black cloud. Oh, God, ahead of him surely was more gold and silver and money than he had ever seen. This was the richest bank outside Mexico City, wasn't it? And now the treasure would be his. He could taste it, it was so close. Smell it. Feel it. He plunged ahead.

A cool blast of air hit him, and he nearly tripped over the remains of the door. He caught himself, then with a surge of energy hurtled through the doorway, arms outstretched to stop him against the safe walls.

His momentum carried him stumbling several feet forward. His hands groped at empty space. More cool air slapped against his face and a blaring light burned away the smoke from his eyes. He stopped suddenly. Something was very wrong.

The last of the smoke cleared away. A high, keening sound escaped him. Something had indeed gone wrong. Very wrong. He wasn't in a safe at all.

He was out in the street.

He realized he was standing in an alley. God, he had made a terrible mistake. He whipped around, expecting to dive back through the smoke into the bank. The safe must still be elsewhere.

A swarm of men rushing through the blasted door stopped him. They were screaming wildly and waving their arms. For the first time, Juan caught the exultant victory, the sense of mad, unleashed conquest in their voices. It was a terrifying sound. He stared at them in fright. What did they want? What would they do now? They seemed mindless, capable of anything. Could they be after him?

He broke from the alley and ran out into a back street. The sun burned overhead. He raced up the street, a steep incline that left him panting at the top. Ahead of him he saw the square where the rebels had been executed by the firing squad. It was empty now. Where should he run?

A group of men turned a corner, spotted him and shouted. They surged toward him, screaming and waving. He turned, seeking escape. More men were approaching from another street.

In terror, he bolted for the only available escape route: a narrow alley to the left. He charged into it, pursued by indistinguishable cries and the pounding of feet. He burst out the other end, only to be jolted to a halt by a rigid, powerful arm.

It was Mallory.

"Where you going?" the Irishman said calmly.

Juan looked frantically behind him. His pursuers were not yet in sight. "The bank, Firecracker," he blurted. "The money." He gasped for breath.

"The bank and the money were transferred to Mexico City over a month ago."

What? What was Mallory saying?

"Since then they've turned the bank into a political prison."

Juan hauled in his breath. A low, guttural moan escaped him. Oh, Christ, he should have realized it. So stupid he was. So blinded by greed. "So that's who . . ." he mumbled tonelessly. Even to himself he sounded defeated.

"Right. They're the one hundred fifty patriots you liberated through 'sheer courage in the face of danger.'" Mallory's tone was mocking him.

The prisoners were coming down the alley, no longer running. They were smiling at him, smiling gratefully he realized now. The sight appalled him.

He grabbed Mallory's collar and twisted. The Irishman's head bent awkwardly to the side. "You knew it," he breathed. "You knew it and you didn't stop me."

Mallory wrenched his head free. "All I asked you was

if you wanted to get inside the bank. I never said anything about money."

Juan raised his pistol. "I'm gonna——"

"You aren't going to do anything. Look!'

The prisoners were almost on him. Behind them more men ran shouting down the alley toward him. He turned. Still more men were converging from three other directions.

With a roar, they *were* on him. He heard Mallory say dryly, "You're a hero of the revolution now!"

Eager hands grabbed him. He felt himself drowning in the hands and in the swollen noise, the screams of lunatics, he thought. He went rigid with terror, felt the hands tighten all over his body, felt the hot breaths of the madmen. He expected to go down, to be crushed into a coffin of hands there on the hard street. His legs gave out and he started to drop. Then suddenly he burst upward into crystal light. The hands dropped away and he saw the world swirling below.

He was on their shoulders, up there under the burning sun in the clean air, being borne like a hero toward the square. Villega was up next to him, waving and calling to the whooping throng below.

Juan looked desperately back toward Mallory, who laughingly shouted at him,

"You're not a bandit any more! You're a revolutionary!"

PART TWO

JOHN

PART TWO

JOHN

Chapter One

"What do you see?"

The woods were hushed and smelled sweetly, almost as if they were touched by the breath of the sea. Mallory thought of dark, cool forests back home. He looked up at Juan and repeated his question.

"Do you see anything?"

Juan was propped high in a tree, his backside against the trunk and his legs braced on a heavy branch. He was peering intently through a spyglass. Mallory had been surprised at the agility with which the beefy Mexican had scaled the tree.

"Well . . . ?" He edged his horse closer.

"Jesus Christ! They look like giant locusts!" Juan called down, awed. "Even the horses got hoods."

"What are you talking about?"

"The soldiers. They're wearing some kind of goggles. Black goggles. And their horses got black hoods." Juan paused. "Yeah, there's lenses in the hoods."

"That's to keep out the dust." Mallory yelled, remembering now that he had seen them before. The British had them too.

"How many soldiers?"

"A full detachment. All cavalry."

"Trucks?"

"Three. No, four. The first one, it's got no windows. It looks like a box on wheels. It's got a machine gun."

"That's the armored car," Mallory said. "Gutierrez should be in it."

Around him, Juan's sons and a half dozen peons, all on horseback, began to murmur about the armored car. Their horses chewed indifferently on leaves from low bushes. Mallory waved them silent.

Juan shifted his position. "There's a man with goggles riding in the turret of the truck," he called. "That's Gutierrez."

"What's he look like?"

"Ugly."

"That could be anybody."

"Yeah. This one's ugly only on one side. He's got a big scar down his face. Makes his mouth look like he's sneering."

"Is he missing an eye?"

Juan didn't answer. He leaned out from the tree. "Yeah," he finally said. "Same side as the scar."

"That's our man. That's the colonel." Mallory said. A light wind rustled the leaves overhead. He felt cool and elated.

"Yeah, well he's pointing in this direction. Now he's bending down and talking to someone inside."

"Put the glass away! He must have seen its reflection."

Juan didn't move. "Hey," he called, "the machine gun's turning this way."

Mallory heard, almost simultaneously, the crisp clatter of the gun and the sound of branches cracking and bending. A shower of leaves rained down from the tree. For a second there was a strange stillness, then another branch snapped and a heavy object thudded to the ground.

Juan picked himself up. He stared mutely at the broken glass in his hand, tossed it aside and reached for his horse. He swung lightly into the saddle.

"Let's go!"

Mallory turned his horse, kicked it, and led the others in a fast gallop deeper into the woods.

They rode for a half hour, exhausting the trail and pushing the horses through tangled underbrush and across twisting streams. The woods closed on them like a door sighing shut on a high dim chamber.

Dusk had already tinged everything gray when they arrived at the camp. Several fires burned low and the smell of cooking hung in the air. Peons in worn clothes were everywhere.

Villega hurried over to them. His eyes flashed excitement but his voice was calm. "Did you find them?" he asked.

Mallory watched Villega intently. He hadn't decided yet about the man. He was passionate, fervid even, in his commitment, and he tempered the passion with careful, thoughtful decisions—a fine leader in that sense. But there was something about him, a hint of softness that Mallory mistrusted. He preferred his leaders totally ruthless; you could always depend on such men.

Juan dismounted. "We found them," he said. "But I think they saw us."

"They saw us." Nino corrected. "They shot at us."

Villega's eyes narrowed. He looked worried. "Were you followed?"

"I don't think so," Juan scratched at his beard. "You got some food for us?"

"Yes, come eat!"

They decided to stay the night where they were. Villega sent out guards to patrol in each direction.

"We'll move in the morning," he said. "If Gutierrez finds us before we're ready, it'll be a slaughter."

Mallory ate slowly, accustoming himself to the flat taste of the maize gruel that the Mexicans called *atole*. He thought of mutton and potatoes and salt fish washed down with whisky. When he finished, he got out his flask and downed a third of it. He would have to settle for gin.

He saw Juan eating across the clearing, joking all the while with two of his sons. Something akin to affection—

perhaps it was just admiration—welled in him. He didn't particularly like the Mexican; he didn't particularly like anyone. But he liked his type. Bloody singleminded, the British would call him. He realized, without fear, that if it ever suited his purpose, the Mexican would kill him with no more scruple than he would feel crushing a bug. And yet he respected the man, crude and scheming though he was. If he weren't so greedy, so damnably determined to enrich Juan and Juan's own and nobody else, he could truly be a hero of the revolution. If he took his enforced role as a revolutionary leader seriously, he'd be a superb guerrilla commander, as cunning as Zapata and as hard and amoral as Villa. And ruthless! He remembered with a grin his enforced march across the desert.

Mallory put away his flask and stretched a blanket under the shelter of a large tree at the edge of the clearing. He wrapped himself in another serape and went off to sleep.

He slept lightly. His ears picked up the twitter of night birds and the crackling of the fire. He awoke at what must have been 1 or 2 A.M. and stared up at a silver sliver, the moon. His mouth was dry.

He heard faint footsteps and turned his head. A large dark shadow glided across the clearing. Juan, unmistakably! The Mexican headed for a cluster of bodies and silently shook them awake. Together they headed off in the direction of the horses.

Mallory rose. The night air was crisp and pleasant. In the distance he could hear the low murmur of a brook. He set out noiselessly after Juan.

The horses were unguarded. Standing in the shadow of a tree, Mallory watched Juan and his gang untie ten of the animals and lead them away from the camp. Their feet crunched dully over the soft ground.

They walked for a half mile. Mallory let them go, wanting to be far out of earshot of the camp before he confronted them. He could not see them in the dark, but he tracked them the way he had learned in Ireland: by their sound, with his head low to the ground.

It was that way that he picked up the intruding noise. He paused. Somewhere nearby a night rodent scratched softly against the ground. Ahead, bushes rustled where Juan and his people walked. A hoof clicked against stone. Beyond that, very faintly, green wood snapped in a fire and the breeze spun in a hollow whisper around a clearing.

Mallory pushed on quickly, circling to Juan's left. The ground swept upward to a knoll. He scrambled to its crest and stopped.

Ahead and slightly to his right he could see the frozen shadows of Juan and his men. They were crouched in the bushes, peering down into the clearing below. The figures of soldiers moving around campfires were clearly visible. A few tents had been set up in the clearing. One of them bore the insignia of a colonel over the door flap, painted large enough to be seen in the dim flickering light of the campfires. Gutierrez?

Mallory heard footsteps crunching along a path and his breath caught. His hand slid silently under his coat. The footsteps came closer. He heard an owl call somewhere far away, and a squad of eight soldiers rushed past. A patrol. The soldiers were muttering something he could not make out. From their haste and the urgency in their voices, he guessed they had found something important. It could be only one thing.

He waited until they were past, then turned and began running back to the rebel campsite. As he turned, he saw Juan and his men crouch lower in the bushes. They too must have heard the oncoming patrol.

Mallory ran as quickly as he could, heedless of stumbling on the rocks underfoot or of crashing into some black tree trunk. Luck and intuition more than the faint moonlight guided him through the dark woods. Thin branches stung his face as he went, and his hands scraped against bark and thorns. He ran loosely, feeling neither excited nor anxious but strangely liberated by the need for haste; a cool pleasure in his own commitment. He wasn't even breathing hard when he got back to the camp.

He found Villega quickly and woke him. Silently, they woke the others. Within minutes they were packed and moving out.

"Aren't you coming?" Villega called.

"In a bit," Mallory said. "Just leave one horse for me."

He found a large, flat rock on the side of the clearing, sat down and waited. He didn't have to wait too long.

Juan and his gang came stumbling into the campsite a few minutes later. Mallory saw Juan's shadowy form stop abruptly and look about in confusion.

"Hey, Papa," Chulo called. "Where'd everybody go?" Juan didn't answer.

A hissing, sizzling light, bright as day, suddenly bathed the clearing. The light arced toward them, growing brighter as it came. For a moment, Juan and his tribe were caught in an eerie tableau, frozen figures staring mutely and increduously up into the sky.

"Duck, you sucker!" Mallory screamed.

Ten bodies dove to the ground. A shell burst loudly overhead and shrapnel showered down, pelting the campsite. The ten bodies wriggled toward the trees. Mallory got up from his rock and calmly walked over to them. He reached into his coat and brought out a bottle as he did.

Juan heard him and looked up, startled.

"That's called shrapnel," Mallory said, uncorking the bottle. "You better get used to it." He tilted the bottle and drank.

Juan started to rise and Mallory tossed the bottle at him. The Mexican caught it, drained the last few drops and flung it into the bushes.

"Let's get out of here," he said.

It rained early the next morning, beginning just before dawn. They had gone about ten miles, and, with the rain falling in great gray sheets, decided to push on a few more miles to a marshy area in the hopes the Gutierrez' trucks would bog down.

Mallory sat under a large canvas stretched between two poles. They had camped in the driest area available, amost a small island in the marsh, but even here the ground was mud. Mallory sat in the mud, reading. He was wearing his black overcoat.

He heard feet sloshing through the muck and looked up at Juan ambling through the dense rain as if he had been born in it. His clothes were totally saturated; his sombrero made its own waterfall.

Juan came under the canvas, gazed curiously at Mallory, then looked toward his half-open suitcase. He went over to the case and pulled out a rolled parchment.

"What's this?" he asked.

Mallory kept reading. "A map," he said.

"Of what?"

"Your country."

"My country is me. ME!! And my sons! And my men!"

Mallory glanced up from the book. "Your country is also Huerta. And the governor. And the landowners. And Gutierrez with his locusts."

Juan shrugged indifferently.

"You don't have anything against them, is that it?" Mallory said. He knew the answer.

"Why should I? They do what they have to. I do what I have to. Everybody's got his place. That's the way life is. The cat chases the mouse. You ever see a mouse chase a cat?"

"If enough mice got together, the cat might come to an inglorious end. Ever think about that?"

Juan smiled wanly. "Firecracker, you think I'm stupid and don't even know what a revolution is. It's a sea of shit. On one side a few people got everything and on the other most people got nothing. Right?"

"Right."

"So the most people make a revolution and kill the others and as soon as they finish, a few sons of bitches take everything and it starts all over again. Right?"

"No," Mallory said slowly. "Actually——"

"Whaddya mean, no? You read books. You tell me if once, just once in this shitty world, if things ain't gone the way I said."

He didn't answer. The rain lightened for a moment and he stared out at a faint rainbow painted just above the treeline far, far off on the horizon. He thought of Ireland, his mind tracking bleakly over the seven years since Arthur Griffith had founded the Sinn Fein. Pain seared through him. What could he say to Juan?

"Go back to your book." The Mexican said.

Mallory slammed it shut. "I already know it by heart." Gutierrez' face flashed before him. He wondered how long it would be before the Mexicans would have to fight him.

Chapter Two

The armored car and the truck were blocking the road. Villega saw them from the top of the low hill but drove on anyway. The small carriage moved lightly ahead, the wheels singing softly. High grass grew along the winding road.

Several soldiers were standing in the road, watching him as he came on. They held their rifles loosely. Villega slowed his horse to a walk and approached the soldiers, looking concerned.

He stopped the carriage thirty feet from the armored car. A soldier with a sodden, stupid face came forward.

"Nobody's allowed through," he said. "The area's being searched."

Villega looked up at the armored car. The machine gun was pointed at him. A hot sun burned overhead. He reached into his pocket and pulled out some papers.

"I have a pass," he said calmly. "I'm a doctor."

The soldier took the papers and examined them skeptically. Ahead, on the roadside, a lieutenant seated on the grass in the shade of a tent eating got up and walked briskly toward them. Another man remained in the tent's shade. Gutierrez. Even from the distance his one eye bored into Villega.

"Where are you going," the lieutenant asked.

"To visit some sick people."

"Their names?"

"Fermin Hernandez, at Chizco. Adelita Aguilar, at Parral . . ." The officer was writing as Villega spoke.

"Isn't there a doctor at Parral?" he asked. His face was hard.

Villega glared at him. "There was," he said, annoyed. "He's been shot."

The officer studied him silently. Villega held his breath. "All right, you may proceed."

An hour later Villega's carriage was tied in a dense wood atop a mountain plateau. The entire valley stretched out lush and green below. Just beneath, a wooden bridge thrust thinly across a narrow river.

Villega stood with Mallory and Juan looking out across the valley. His thin face was lined and there were dark rings under his eyes that hadn't been there before. Farther back in the trees a dozen peons stood by loaded burros. Juan's own people milled about listlessly.

"Gutierrez is less than twenty miles from here, on the road to the San Jorge Bridge," Villega said wearily, pointing to the bridge. "They'll comb the area bush by bush. That's why the order is to split up and try to save yourselves individually."

A thin breeze stirred the leaves overhead. "What a brilliant order," Mallory said bitterly. "We're up to our asses in mud back in the marshes and the rest of you are in a warm basement."

Villega looked wounded. "Not everybody can fight," he said, frowning. "There are those who must organize, coordinate——"

"Yes, sure. Don't pay any attention to me, it's personal."

Mallory walked away. He headed for two rebels busy unloading a dismantled machine gun from a burro. Saying nothing, he waved the men aside and swung his arm around the gun's barrel. With his free hand he caught the tripod.

He carried the gun back to Juan and Villega. "Sorry about the orders," he said, "but I'm staying."

The two Mexicans gaped at him. Mallory squatted and began assembling the gun. A fly spun past his head and he swatted it away. He said slowly, not looking up, his voice tight with anger, "I don't give a bloody fuck about your revolution. I'm not even sure I care about my own any more. It's just that at a certain point, a man gets tired of tramping around the mountains, so he stops."

He tightened a screw on the gun. "Well, I'm stopping here. At the San Jorge Bridge. Why? Maybe because my feet are sore."

Finished, he stood up. He gazed coolly at the two Mexicans. To his surprise Juan announced, "If he stays, I stay, too." There was a calculating gleam in his eye.

"What? What the hell for?" Villega demanded.

Juan shrugged. "My feet hurt, too."

He wheeled and marched quickly toward the rebels. Since Mesa Verde, to Mallory's great amusement, they had regarded Juan as second only to Villega.

"Hey," Juan called. "Listen to me."

The men looked up.

"Me and Irish we've decided to catch us a few of them locusts. The rest of you get behind that hill over there and wait for us. And if you see things getting bad up here, beat it. Every man for himself."

He paused. There were no complaints, only admiring stares. "Okay," he barked. "Now move your asses."

Grim-faced, Juan approached his sons. They looked at him icily. Mallory regarded them with interest. Whatever Juan was selling, they clearly weren't buying. They knew their father too well: The unselfish hero mantle didn't fit him.

"My sons," Juan said grandly. "You go too. And if your father doesn't come back . . ." His voice choked.

The boys remained expressionless. There was a moment's silence, then the *niños* turned and, heads down, obediently moved away. Nino, Fefe, and Amando trotted after them. They retreated deeper into the woods, not following the rebels around the slope of the hill.

Mallory hadn't been able to see Juan's face when he spoke to his sons, but he would have bet all the money in Dublin that Juan had been winking furiously at them. The whole thing stank like a penny whore's breath. Those boys so docile in the face of that comedy? Not likely. Mallory shook his head and glanced at Villega. The whole act had clearly been meant for him and his rebels. The doctor seemed genuinely moved. Well, it had worked on someone.

Villega untied his carriage and climbed in. He threw a good luck gesture to Juan, another to Mallory, then drove off. His carriage wound down the path and disappeared among the trees.

Mallory moved the machine gun forward to the edge of the plateau. He braced it against a flat stone, in a spot shielded by thick trees, and trained the barrel down on the bridge. He was pleased with the angle and the cover. It would be a good fight.

He rose and took out his flask. The retreating figures of Juan's men could be seen moving quickly toward the next hill.

Juan smiled at him.

"As soon as they get over the hill. Okay?" he said.

Mallory cocked his eyebrows quizzically.

"That's when we run for it. Okay?"

The Irishman pulled silently on his flask.

"No?"

Mallory didn't answer.

"You mean you're serious about staying here?"

Mallory nodded. He took a last swallow and slid the flask back under his overcoat.

"Motherofjesus! All those explosions must have destroyed your brain," Juan hissed. He ran his hand through thick, oily hair and sighed. "I was sure it was a trick so we could get the hell out of here."

Mallory shrugged and turned away.

"Goddamnit, why the hell you think I stayed here with you except to get rid of Villega and those idiot revolutionaries who keep following me around? Did you think I wanted to fight the locusts? Are you crazy? The two of us against all of them?"

Far down the valley something black was snaking slowly along the road to the bridge. Mallory studied it intently.

"Listen, Firecracker. Let's get out of here. We can still get rich on the banks in America. Think of all those millions."

The black object began to take shape. Trucks and massed troops.

"Listen," Mallory said slowly. "If you go you'd be doing me a great favor. If I have to choose between being a thief or a revolutionary, even in someone else's revolution, I'll take the job I know best. You can still get out of here in time."

Juan spat on the ground. "Your mother was a donkey and your father was a horse," he snapped. He began pacing furiously back and forth, scowling at the bridge below. Finally, he stopped. "I'm staying," he shouted. "You tight-assed know-it-all Irish piece of shit, you ain't the only man alive with two balls."

Radiating anger, he stomped over to Mallory's suitcase, laying half opened under a tree, and took out a pair of binoculars clearly visible in a corner of the case. Mallory eyed him curiously. Juan marched directly to the machine gun, sat down before it and stared stonily down at the bridge.

"They'll be coming off it almost facing you," Mallory said. "Cover their front. I'll get them from behind."

He walked lightly toward the burros, feeling exactly nothing about the coming fight except a detached awareness of its necessity. Either they got Gutierrez or he would get them. To continue running and hiding was stupid. You had to fight sometime in a war.

He unstrung another machine gun, shouldered it and returned to grab up his suitcase. With the gun and the case, he carefully slid down the hill to the bridge.

Why hadn't he fled with Juan, he wondered? Why hadn't he taken a dozen opportunities to quit the rebels? He shifted the gun on his shoulder. His heels bit into the dirt. Probably for no better reason than he had said; what else did he know? Now that there was no job for him in Mexico, what else was he to do? Who could he feel comfortable among except the rebels? Besides, he was a wanted man. So he really had no choice. Since he hadn't any, he might as well do a proper job of being a revolutionary.

He was still thinking about it as he prepared for Gutierrez.

Chapter Three

Somewhere nearby a wasp droned steadily. A swarm of gnats swam in front of Juan and he brushed them away. He raised the glasses and looked across the valley. The armored car was clearly visible, churning up a low cloud of dust as it came. A man was riding in the turret. He supposed it was the colonel.

He swung the glasses down to the long, narrow bridge. He could see every splinter in the wood. The water beneath it looked cool and blue. Weeds grew along the river bank.

He looked for Mallory. The Irishman was beneath him and to the left, just now positioning himself behind a rock at the bottom of the hill. At that spot, he was actually below the bridge. From there, unseen, he could sweep the approaches.

Juan wiped his sweating palms on his pants. The sun had swung behind him. Free of the treeline, it was searing his back.

"What the hell am I doing here?" he mumbled to himself. "What do I care about the revolution?"

He should get out. He wanted to. But the thought of abandoning Mallory, of abandoning any hope of taking a big bank, kept him frozen. Who could tell what opportunities fate would bring?

He studied Mallory through the glasses. A ridiculous figure, sitting down there in that black coat and bowler with a machine gun propped in front of him. In Ireland . . . maybe. In Mexico . . . well. In Mexico revolutions weren't fought that way.

He watched as Mallory drank deeply from his flask and put it away. The Irishman lay back and flipped his bowler over his eyes. He was going to sleep. To sleep?

"I'm getting out of here," Juan muttered, but he didn't move. It must be the heat, he thought.

On the ground nearby a large black ant was struggling with a red insect twice its size. The ant had the squirming insect locked in its jaws and was carrying it back toward its nest. It staggered forward and was spun around by a violent thrust from the insect. The ant stumbled, regained its balance and plodded another few steps before it was thrown back again. The pattern continued.

Juan observed the drama dazedly. Hot air swung around his head and his eyes glazed over. He felt his body sag, and he shook his head to clear it. His mouth was dry.

Another violent kick sent the ant onto its back. It lay there with the bigger, heavier insect still squirming in its jaws, unable to right itself against the weight but unwilling to let go. Long minutes plodded by. Juan watched until it appeared both insects would die in their futile struggle, then he reached out and crushed them.

His head drooped. Sweat collected at his neck and ran down his back. The air seemed to shimmer before him and his mind spun off to another place.

When he looked up the troops were gone.

The road clear down the valley was empty. He looked at the bridge. Nothing. He gazed out at the road again. Only one part of it was blocked to his view and that was very near. A low, flat hill obscured the road there. But Gutierrez couldn't have come that close. Not enough time had passed.

He stared at the point of the road curving out from the hill. His ears primed for the sound of motors. He heard a bird flutter nearby and caught the soft surge of the stream below. And then, faintly, something else.

The head of the armored car loomed blackly at the curve of the road and rolled slowly, relentlessly toward him. Behind it, a seemingly endless column of forces emerged from the back side of the hill. Like a great train, the column swept toward him.

"Motherofjesus," Juan gasped. "The locusts!"

In awe, he raised the glasses and peered down at the troops. In the turret of the armored car was the unmistakable face of Gutierrez. He was surveying the terrain ahead with his one, expert eye. Sweat glistened on his hard face.

The column crawled on toward the bridge as Juan stared in mute fascination through the glasses. Near the entrance, so close now that he felt he could reach down and touch it, the armored car pulled to the side of the road. Gutierrez waved one truck to the head of the column and positioned the other two on the bridge approach. A shouted order sent men scrambling to man the guns on the trucks.

Juan watched in dismay. The man was uncanny to suspect something. He must be in touch with the saints. He looked frantically down at Mallory. Incredibly, the Irishman was still asleep. Still asleep? He glanced anxiously back up at the troops. The lead truck was edging its way onto the bridge, with the cavalrymen following warily behind. The truck was coming directly toward him.

Enraged, he grabbed a rock and flung it down the hill at Mallory. It fell short. He reached for another and arched it even higher. It too fell short.

Cursing and hissing, his hands tightened on the machine gun. Screw Irish. He would fight them himself. He glared at the oncoming truck. It was halfway across the bridge. He swung the gun toward it.

At the bottom of his vision he glimpsed Mallory stir. Juan checked the desire to call out. Get up you bastard, he screamed silently. Get up!

A hand came up and raised the bowler. Juan heard the truck change gears. He caught his breath. Hurry up, you Irish whore, he thought. The truck came closer.

Mallory rose to a sitting position. He looked up to Juan and waved to him coolly: Everything's okay.

Juan's face convulsed in anger. For a moment he considered shooting the Irishman. He kept the gun trained on the lead truck.

The truck was near the end of the bridge. Mallory's arm went up suddenly and swept sharply downward in a signal to fire. Juan squeezed the trigger, bracing himself for the rattle of the gun.

Nothing happened. His hand tightened again and he feverishly shook the weapon. Still nothing. His mind raced. Why had it jammed? What would he do now?

The truck was at the end of the bridge. The sun reflected off the windshield, shooting darts of colored light back up to him. He stared blindly into the light; it was all he could see. His eyes widened and he tried to shoot the light away.

The gun went off with a clatter, pounding his elbows into his body. He took the shock with pleasure and felt the gun hammering in his hands.

The truck's windshield shattered and the darts of light disappeared. Juan saw glass fragments fly away and glimpsed for a second the terrified, bloody face of the driver. Then the truck swerved sharply to the right and stopped with a jolt against the stone abutment at the edge of the bridge. It was now obstructing the end of the span.

Trapped on the bridge behind the truck, the cavalrymen looked up helplessly in the direction of the chattering gun. Their horses kicked and bounced against each other. Frantically, the soldiers tried to turn the animals. Their cries drifted up to Juan.

The troops at the rear managed to come about and head back toward the armored car. Mallory caught them a moment into their desperate retreat, firing his gun into the lead horses as they bolted from the bridge. The horses crumpled and fell into pools of their own blood. Their riders staggered up and lurched toward the shelter of the armored car. Mallory cut them down.

Juan heard Gutierrez screaming unintelligibly as he turned his gun on the head of the column. Mercilessly, he let the weapon chew at the troops at his end of the bridge while Mallory swept the far end. Slowly and inexorably, as if they were burning a string at both ends, they were destroying the column.

Bleating fearfully, the horses bucked and reared, kicking and stomping men thrown to the ground. Blood spurted everywhere, splashing vivid red stains along the planking. The troops in the middle of the bridge panicked.

In terror, trapped amid frenzied horses and the relentless machine-gun fire, they began shooting their own animals. The survivors crawled under the arches of the bridge, seeking some shelter.

A piece of bark flew from a tree near Juan's head. Dust and pebbles sprayed upward from the ground beside him. He looked toward the armored car. A machine gun was firing blindly at him, raking the trees.

In the turret Gutierrez was still shouting orders. "Fire! Fire! Fire!" he screamed to his gunners. He turned to the cavalrymen. "Get under the bridge! Under the bridge. Hurry, under the bridge." His voice held a thin edge of hysteria.

Juan's hands burned. The gun, now almost stove-hot, jumped madly in his hands. He loosened his grip. His arms ached and his eyes burned and his head swam fiercely as hot blood pounded into it. No more than fifteen seconds had passed since he had begun firing.

Down below now troops were jumping from the parapets into the water or onto the river banks. The truck guns were spewing bullets at an incredible rate, eating away the foliage in a huge swath around Juan. He saw the armored car rumble toward the bridge for a better angle, Gutierrez still yelling commands from atop.

Juan hunched down and fired wildly. They would have

to get the trucks soon. They were being outgunned. Any moment, someone might get lucky.

He looked for Mallory. The Irishman had stopped shooting. What? Why? What was he doing?

Mallory reached behind a rock on his left. A detonating box came out in his hand. Juan braced even as Mallory casually pushed down the handle.

The explosion was monstrous. It hurled the bridge's midsection forty feet in the air, where it burst apart like a bomb. A black cloud mushroomed up beneath the debris even before it hit the ground.

Stunned, Juan stopped shooting. Wave after wave of burning air beat against his face. Dust swirled into his nose and eyes. Armies clashed in his head.

The smoke turned milky gray. It rose slowly from between the river banks. Blackened rubble and jagged heaps of wood and metal now stretched the full width of the shallow stream, blocking it. Only an occasional arm or leg protruded lifelessly from the debris. The other soldiers who had been on the bridge couldn't be seen at all.

On the far bank one of the trucks burned fiercely. The other stood twisted and useless, its guns silent. Next to it lay the armored truck. It had overturned.

A few dazed survivors staggered helplessly about through the dense smoke. Everything else was still. Juan heard only the faint lapping of the water against the ruins of the bridge. He sighed. He wondered if Gutierrez was among the survivors.

Mallory clambered up the hill toward him carrying the suitcase and the machine gun. His expression told Juan nothing. He was walking slowly, gazing straight ahead. At most, he seemed pensive.

He reached the top, paused, then walked stiffly past Juan without looking at him.

"Don't kill them," he said as he passed.

"It never crossed my mind," Juan replied.

Chapter Four

The celebration was over. A few men sat warming themselves at the fires, but most slept drunkenly under their serapes. Empty bottles and leftover food littered the cave floor.

A record player was droning out a sleepy Mexican love song. In a corner, a small, wiry peon slumped against a rock, picking langorously on a guitar in tune to the music. The notes echoed crisply in the cavernous chamber.

Mallory sat on a blanket far back in the cave, only dimly aware of the music. His hands held a book of speeches by Herzen, but he wasn't reading. A snapshot of Juan sleeping across the way with a smile on his face, of Sebastian digging salt out of a box for his tequilla, and of old Nino lighting a cigar with trembling fingers hung before him like images on a transparent silkscreen. He was casually aware of the images, but he was looking beyond them. Beyond them he saw only colored lights.

The music stopped and a figure moved toward the record player. A hush settled over the cave. There was the sound of a record scratching, and a slow, mournful Irish tune filled the chamber.

Mallory turned toward the Gramophone. The machine's image hovered on the silkscreen but beyond it now the colored lights were beginning to take form. Trees and fences and low rolling hills of deep green appeared in a strange, filtered light. The Irish countryside.

On the silkscreen Juan stirred, sat up, listened to the

music a moment, then rose and approached Mallory. Silently, he held out a bottle of whisky. Mallory reached out automatically and drank. He stared blankly past Juan, as the green countryside came sharply to life.

The spinning wheels of an automobile on a white dust road rolled into view. The polished machine was framed against high grass. In the front seat a girl in a lemon dress with flowing dark hair sat between two young men.

Mallory saw the girl's lovely, fresh face and the boyish, exultant look of Nolan, his friend, and he saw faintly his own lean young face, exuberant and carefree. Nolan was driving. They passed a bottle back and forth between them and took turns kissing the girl. They were all laughing and happy.

A terrible, burning pain rushed through him. He drained the bottle and flung it hard toward the Gramophone. It shattered against the turntable. A screech pierced the cavern as the needle cut across the record.

Mallory got up and went over to the Gramophone. The record lay broken in a dozen fragments. He looked dully up at Juan and Villega, who had emerged from the shadows at the front of the cave.

"It slipped," he said.

"What a shame. I had such a hard time finding it," Villega said lightly. He bent and picked up a piece. He shrugged. "Well, I understand. It's been a hard day. You started off with sore feet and—" Villega smiled at Juan. "And if they stay sore, we could arrive in Mexico City before Pancho Villa."

"Is that where we're supposed to be going?" Mallory asked moodily.

"Well, that's where Villa's going."

"What about us?"

"I'm not certain yet what our role will be."

"Yeah, when *will* you know?" Mallory's mouth tasted sour.

"In a day or so. When I come back I hope I can bring

good news about the advance of the revolutionary army.
And our orders. We should be moving out of here very
soon."

Juan shifted uneasily. Mallory ignored him.

"Who's winning this fucking war anyway?" he said.

"We are, of course," Villega grunted.

"Okay, then tell whoever it is you tell that they should
get their asses moving and get it over with."

Villega started to answer, checked himself, nodded and
left. Mallory found himself thinking he had sounded like
a fool. He hadn't done much to bring his own revolution
home to victory; he shouldn't be so arrogant and impa-
tient with the Mexicans. Huerta was smart and tough. No
army of peasants would defeat him easily. Still, they cer-
tainly wouldn't beat him if they kept hidden in marshes
and caves. They had to fight. The bridge was proof enough
of that.

He heard Villega's carriage pulling away. In a day or
so, the doctor had said. In Ireland, they would bet their
lone pair of wool socks against it. No, Villega would go to
Mesa Verde and talk to his people again and consult with
Villa's emissaries, then come back and report that the time
was not yet right. They were not strong enough. They
would have to wait for more propitious circumstances or
until the Mesa Verde garrison was diverted to Mexico
City or until . . .

Mallory thought about going after Villega, inviting himself to the strategy session in Mesa Verde. He shrugged
off the notion and went over and lay down on a straw
mat in the corner. To interfere would only breed resentment, he told himself. Grappling with his own uneasiness,
he slipped off to a fitful sleep.

He was awakened several hours later by alarmed cries
from a young boy.

An hour out of Mesa Verde, Villega pulled off the road
onto a narrow path and followed it through high grass for

a mile. Ahead of him loomed the shadowy form of a farmhouse, lit only by the stars. The man who owned it was a sympathizer. His house was used as a way station for messages between Mesa Verde and the rebels in the Sierras. It was never wise to enter the city without first checking for warning messages.

Villega tied his horse and walked toward the blackened house. Pablo and his young brother would be sleeping. No matter, they would not mind being wakened.

He lifted the door latch and went in. He felt on his right for the candle. It was in its usual place. Villega lighted it. "Pablo," he called.

He took a step into the room. "Oh, my God," he said.

Pablo lay on his bed, staring sightlessly into the air. What remained of his face was covered with blood. The sheets twisted over his body were dark and wet.

"We were expecting you, Doctor," a voice behind him announced.

Villega whirled. Gutierrez, his lieutenant, and four soldiers stepped out of the shadows. The colonel's empty eye socket watered obscenely in the flickering candle light.

In a moment they were on him. Strong hands gripped him and pulled him out the door. The soldiers tied his arms behind him, punching him as they did. Then they threw him into the back of the carriage and drove off. He passed out a few minutes later.

He didn't come to until they were back in Mesa Verde, within the walls of the garrison. The soldier dragged him into a dank stone building and down a stone staircase into a bare cellar. An iron door clanked shut at the top of the steps.

A kerosene lantern hung by a long chain from the ceiling, swaying slightly, casting a bleak, cold light. On the walls the soldiers' shadows loomed monstrously large and foreboding.

"What do you want with me?" Villega said in a complaining tone. It was difficult keeping his voice from shaking.

A smile edged Gutierrez's taut face. "You'll see in a while," he said.

The soldiers stripped off his shirt and tied him to one of the two chairs in the room. His blood raced madly and he suppressed the insane desire to cry out for help. He knew what was about to happen. He feared only the consequences.

He sat in silence in the cool, gloomy cellar while the soldiers went away briefly. They returned with their jackets off, carrying short, heavy clubs.

"Oh, no!!!"

They beat him first on the neck and back, then worked at his chest and stomach. Each blow to his frail body brought a gasp. They beat him methodically, saying nothing, two of them hitting him at a time. After the first four blows, he didn't believe he could endure any more pain. After the first ten, he was screaming silently for them to stop. Every blow after that lost its distinctiveness; it no longer felt as if he was being hit by clubs; rather his whole body was being slammed between two huge steel plates.

"That's enough!"

Through half-closed eyes he could see Gutierrez' impassive face hove into view. "That was just to prepare you," he said coldly. "Now I want you to tell me the name of every revolutionary in Mesa Verde and the location of your mountain hideout. You will tell me now."

Villega said nothing.

Gutierrez reached out and jerked his head upward by the hair. "You know you will be beaten until you tell me, don't you?"

Villega nodded.

"Well?"

With what strength he could muster, Villega tore his hair from Gutierrez's grasp.

"Beat him!" the colonel snapped.

The soldiers used the blunt end of their clubs this time, driving them into his belly and groin. He writhed in pain. Tears welled in his eyes. He moaned and cried out. They hit him again and again. The pain consumed him, and he began to whimper. He wanted so badly to die.

At last they stopped. Mercifully, his mind had begun to detach itself from his body, drifting off to a nightmarish swill where nausea and agony were the perpetual terms of existence, to be endured dully and in silence.

Water splashed his face. He shook his head and looked glassily at Gutierrez, seated before him now.

"Kill me!" he gasped. "Kill me! I won't tell you anything. Kill me!"

"Are you certain, Doctor?"

He nodded faintly.

Gutierrez smiled. "You'll talk, Villega. You'll talk. Do you know why? Because you are too intelligent not to. You have imagination, and imagination is the enemy of courage."

He motioned to a soldier. "Look over there, Doctor," he said.

The soldier was coming toward him slowly. Held before him was a pair of plyers. "Noooo—" Villega cried.

"Tell me!"

"I can't," he whined pathetically. "I can't."

"Yes, you can."

Gutierrez' chair scraped on the floor and he disappeared from view. Villega saw the soldier bend behind him with the pliers. He gritted his teeth as the pliers clamped around his nipple.

And then he screamed inhumanly.

Chapter Five

The corpse was stiff and already had the grayish-blue color of death. Mallory pulled a blanket over the pulpy face and turned to the boy, who had refused to come closer.

"How much time has gone by?" he asked.

"The time for me to get to you and bring you here."

They had left immediately after the boy woke them. He and Juan had pushed their horses hard, and the boy had proven to be a competent rider. "More than six hours," Mallory muttered, mostly to himself.

He looked at Juan. "I'm going to Mesa Verde. Maybe there's still time to help the doctor."

Juan sighed. "Okay . . . let's go," he said resignedly.

"I said *I'm* going."

He moved toward the door. Behind him Juan called, "Wait. When will you be back?"

"When you see me."

Juan followed him out. "And if I don't see you?"

"If you don't see me, stick a chili pepper up your ass and run like you've never run before. And don't look over your shoulder, there'll be soldiers behind you."

The road was clear all the way to Mesa Verde. It surprised him. Several times he pulled his horse to a standstill, just to listen. But there was nothing. Not even a patrol. Perhaps something important was happening in the city. Could Villega have talked? Would he have told them where the hideout was?

It was 3 A.M. when he reached the city, and it was raining. He knew instantly something was wrong. There were lights in one or two outlying houses when there shouldn't have been, not at that hour. And as he neared the main section of the city, he could hear the distant whine of truck engines. There could be only one reason for that many trucks, to move troops.

He left his horse tied in an alleyway and made on foot for the spot where the trucks seemed to be, keeping to the shadows. If he were spotted he would have to run; there would be no way to explain his presence in the streets at that time of morning.

He wasn't spotted. A patrol passed by at one point, but he crouched behind a rain barrel at the side of a house until it was gone. It felt strange. How many times had he done the same thing in Dublin?

The trucks seemed to be in or near the square. The best vantage point would be from the north; that section offered the most concealment. He circled several blocks out of his way, cutting round the square at a safe distance, until he was able to approach it through a back alleyway and slip behind a column to a small government building.

The trucks were indeed there. They were lined up one hundred feet from a wall painted with white stripes, their acetylene headlights hissing softly in the rain. The lights made the wall bright as day.

The square was filled with troops. Some stood grimly around the trucks while the others came and went in small groups, marching determinedly. Four men stood shivering in front of the striped wall, a squad of soldiers guarding them. The men kept darting fearful looks from the soldiers to a small cluster of women who stood huddled at the other side of the square, surrounded by troops as well. The heads of the women were uncovered despite the rain. Mallory could hear them sobbing. One of the women cried out, and a guard moved in front of her, blocking Mallory's view. The woman fell silent. Whatever the guard had said had been effective.

He saw a small platoon come up from the south, dragging a man who was wearing only pants. Even his feet were bare. The soldiers pulled the man across the square and stopped in front of one of the trucks, the headlight shining full on his face. Mallory recognized him. He had seen him that day in the tavern basement.

A slim, erect figure came out from between two trucks and stepped in front of the light. It was Gutierrez. The colonel walked over to the man and harshly lifted his face up toward the cab, as if to show it to someone sitting inside the truck. Mallory squinted in the rain and tried to see inside. The windows reflected only the light from the other trucks.

Gutierrez nodded, and the troops dragged the man toward the wall. "Oh, no," he whimpered. "Don't do it." But they ignored him.

More squads were arriving now, each with a prisoner in tow. They all followed the same pattern, stopping for a moment before the headlights while Gutierrez looked up at whoever was inside and then passed judgment. Out of two dozen men, Mallory counted only three who were freed. Several of those who weren't he knew from the tavern.

Gutierrez barked an order and a line of soldiers quickly formed in front of the wall. The prisoners cowered together, the bluish acetylene light making their expressions look overwhelmingly pathetic. They were shoved roughly apart and forced back against the wall. The women began wailing, and not even the angry growls of the soldiers silenced them now. The prisoners looked pitifully over at the women. Though their tears were invisible in the rain, Mallory could tell that a few of the men had begun to cry.

"Attention!" Gutierrez barked, and the firing squad straightened. "Ready!" The soldiers brought their guns up. Gutierrez' expression was the same as ever, the scar forcing his mouth into an ugly sneer. "Aim!" The soldiers sighted down the barrel. The keening of the women grew sharper. Mallory looked toward the truck windows. The only thing he could see was the relentless metronome of the windshield wipers.

The silkscreen suddenly snapped down in front of his eyes again. On the surface, frozen in tableau, were the soldiers with their rifles poised and the swishing wipers and the men against the wall. Behind it all, Mallory was seeing something else.

He was in a pub. Dublin it was. The place was crowded and noisy, filled with young, animated people. The yellow light from gas lanterns softened their features and made them all look a little drunk. Whisky and dark beer were being swilled in great quantities, amid laughter, argument, and good cheer.

Mallory was sitting at the bar, drinking beer and peering through the smoke at nothing in particular. Before him on the bar lay a rolled-up newspaper. An Irish melody tinkled from a piano in the background.

There was a crash. The music stopped and the crowd fell silent. Mallory turned slowly and looked toward the door. British troops were rushing in, pushing people aside with their rifles. Their uniforms marked them as members of the Black and Tan Corps. The drinkers froze and stared in hostility at the troops. Three soldiers placed themselves to cover the room. Mallory turned away.

An English officer with a gaunt, pockmarked face came in behind the soldiers, pushing ahead of him a civilian in torn clothes. The man kept his head down, concealing his face. The officer stopped and looked icily at the customers, then prodded the civilian, who hesitantly lifted an arm and pointed to a man seated at the bar. Immediately several soldiers fell on him and hustled him out. No one said a word.

The officer guided his charge down through the pub. Mallory watched in the foggy mirror behind the bar as the civilian pointed out one man after another for the soldiers to drag away.

They stopped a few feet from Mallory. In the mirror he could see the officer stare stonily at his back and prod the civilian again, even harder. Reluctantly, the man raised his head. Through the smoke Mallory saw the cut and bruised face of Nolan, the boy who had been in the car with him. Nolan, his best friend.

Their eyes met in the mirror in grim recognition and held for a moment. Nolan's were dull with shame. He looked away in dismay.

The officer caught it all. He pointed to Mallory's back and snapped an order. On either side of Mallory, customers moved rapidly away.

He waited until the soldiers were almost upon him. Then he grabbed up the rolled newspaper and spun quickly around. He killed the officer first and then the soldiers. Nolan he shot last.

"Fire!" Gutierrez barked, and the crack of the rifles echoed sharply through the square.

The men against the wall fell in a heap. Their bodies lay on the wet ground while the rain washed silently over them.

Mallory glanced again at the truck. Pressed against the windshield, palled in horror, was the battered face of Villega. The face disappeared into the darkness of the truck cab a moment later.

Gutierrez climbed into another truck, and it pulled away. One by one the other vehicles followed. In the dimming light, Mallory noticed that a few lingering soldiers were over by the bodies, kicking at them. Anyone who seemed still alive, they shot with their pistols.

He ran for his horse, disdaining the shadows. If they saw him now, they'd have to be quick to kill him. Otherwise they could chase him as far as they wanted; what did it matter now? He couldn't lead them anywhere they didn't know about already.

An hour out of town he saw the first flares soaring above the mountains. Oh God, they were there already. They must have moved out a large force even while the other troops began the search through Mesa Verde for the rebel suspects. They would have taken the Aguadiz road, knowing that the main road, the one he was on, might be watched. Otherwise they had been smugly confident; Gutierrez remaining behind was proof of that. He wondered if the sentries had spotted the troops in time to give warning.

Even before he reached the farmhouse he knew they hadn't. The flares were bursting feverishly in the inky distance, splashing the dark, cloudy sky with dull pastels. And beneath them, lower to the ground, there were flames.

As he neared the farmhouse, he saw Juan's bulky form run out and jump on a horse. The Mexican wasn't taking any chances. Mallory called to him, and Juan held his horse in rein.

"Well? What happened?" Juan asked when Mallory stopped beside him.

"You can see for yourself."

Juan worriedly followed his gaze toward the glowing flares. "What's happening up there, Irish?"

"Anything but fireworks."

"It looks . . . it looks like our side . . ." Juan muttered. It was the first time Mallory had ever detected anxiety in the Mexican's voice.

"Pretty hard to judge from this distance," he said.

Juan threw him a pained look and kicked his horse. Mallory galloped off after him. He saw Villega's ghastly face all through the ride into the mountains.

Chapter Six

"We'd better go the rest of the way on foot."

They were in a thicket a half mile from the cave. A gray, somber dawn had begun to edge its way along the horizon, but there was still enough darkness to conceal them. The woods smelled fresh and wet, though it had not rained in the mountains.

They crept forward slowly. The last flares had burned out two hours earlier, and the stillness had increased their apprehension as they rode. Now it made them suspicious. There was nothing to be heard but night sounds.

They stopped every ten feet and listened. Nothing. Could the troops have gone or were they lying in ambush? Mallory hoped they were out still chasing the rebels, but he knew the wish was a lie. The flares told him that.

"Over there," Juan whispered, pointing.

On the ground a dozen feet away lay a hat which looked strangely familiar. They moved toward it, and Juan bent and picked it up. It was Nino's.

Juan looked anxiously around. A shadowy form lay half-concealed by a bush. He rushed to it and brushed back the leaves. Even from where he stood Mallory could see it was the old man.

Nino had no stomach left. It had been blown away by a shot fired from very close on. The old man had died instantly.

Mallory looked at Juan. Except for the slight flaring of

his nostrils and his bloodless lips, his face showed nothing. Juan turned away and moved grimly toward the cave.

The last gasp of the moon showed them a deserted clearing in front of the cave. They crouched behind some bushes and waited. A moment later, from below, came a faint metallic clicking and the muffled whinny of a horse.

"They're down along the road," Mallory whispered. "They must figure that whoever would come to the cave would come up along the road. Besides, it gives them better cover."

"Maybe they left somebody in the cave."

"I don't know. Be careful."

They edged along the outsides of the clearing, heading for the mouth of the cave. Juan stopped suddenly. Ahead, propped against a rock, was the body of a peon, his face grotesquely contorted in pain. He had been shot in the neck and had obviously died slowly, the blood running down into his lap.

Juan straightened. In anguish, he stepped out into the clearing and moved quickly toward the cave, indifferent now to any danger. Mallory watched from behind some trees. It was better, he thought, to leave Juan alone. If there were soldiers in there, they would have found out soon enough anyway.

Juan disappeared inside. Mallory waited, and when nothing happened, edged closer. Down below a horse snorted. It was the only sound.

The moon slipped behind some clouds again and darkness blanketed the clearing. Mallory stepped to the side of the cave entrance and leaned back against the wall, into the shadows. There was nothing to do but wait.

He didn't know how much time had passed, though it couldn't have been much, when Juan came out. He was walking woodenly, his eyes vacant. A machine gun and some belts of ammunition were under his arm. Mallory moved up beside him. The Mexican didn't even look his way.

They stood there for long moments, saying nothing. Juan was breathing deeply, hauling the air in loudly and letting it go in short, fitful bursts. It wasn't much but it told Mallory all he had to know.

He didn't ask. He waited for Juan to say it. When he finally did, Juan's voice was dull and distant, the voice of a man not hearing his own words. "All of them, Irish," he breathed. "All six."

He calmly lowered the machine gun to his hands and began loading it. Mallory touched his arm. "They're waiting for somebody down there," he said, "You won't really get them by surprise."

"I know."

"Let me get some dynamite, first."

"No. This time I do it my way."

It was a kind of madness he had known before. They always wrote about it in books about wars; that point beyond fear when the only thing to be done was the stupid thing: there were no other options. Mallory watched Juan disappear into the darkness, then turned toward the cave.

The first body was ten feet inside, a peon shot before he could reach his gun. The weapon leaned against the cave wall, the dead man's hands only inches from it.

The rest of it didn't surprise him. The inside of the cave was littered with their bodies. Only a few had been able to get to their weapons before the soldiers pouring in had cut them down. Most of them must have died quickly in that first assault, not knowing what had happened until it was too late.

He saw Chulo first. His small body was tightly balled in a fetal position with his arms across his chest. The body was lying across the chalky ember of a fire. The boy appeared to have been wounded in the diaphragm. He would have died in agonizing pain, gasping for air.

Juan's other children were scattered around the dim chamber. Sebastian, the oldest, was over by the smashed

Gramophone. In death, he had aged immensely. He looked more like his father than ever, Mallory thought.

Benito, who was what . . . all of fourteen? . . . was the worst of them. His face had been shot away and someone had stepped on his hand, pancaking it to the ground.

In the near distance Mallory heard the chatter of machine guns followed by faint shouts. Juan was on them. Or they were on him. Mallory stared down at Benito and found himself suddenly wanting badly to join the Mexican.

Mallory moved quickly toward the rear entrance to the cave. It brought him out on a knoll overlooking the road down below. The shooting had stopped. The wind woofed up from below, carrying the muted sounds of scuffling and of orders being snapped. In the gray darkness he could make out some vague, thrashing forms. A struggling figure was lifted up and carried away. It could have only been Juan.

So they had captured him. Gutierrez' orders would have been to take alive any late visitors to the cave. Presumably they would have either emissaries from Villa or messengers from Mesa Verde who might lead them to any remnants of the rebel network. That meant they'd bring Juan back to Mesa Verde for questioning. When they discovered he didn't know anything, they'd shoot him.

There was only one thing to do.

He went back into the cave and searched for his suitcase. It was gone. The soldiers hadn't minded leaving a few weapons around, but they weren't going to be generous with explosives. The death smell unnerved him, and he went outside again and sat down on a rock.

There'd be no chance to free Juan now or on the ride back to Mesa Verde, not without explosives. His only chance would be in the city. If they took Juan to the garrison, he might catch them off guard: familiar surroundings always relaxed men and made them careless. If not there, then perhaps while they were taking him to be shot.

Mallory returned to his horse and led it to a point where he could overlook the road into the cave. It was growing lighter now, the beginning of a thick, sullen day. He waited until a platoon of a dozen soldiers rode out with Juan and watched to see which road they took to Mesa Verde. They were going by the main road. Mallory chose the Aguadiz route.

The ride back was interminable. The horse was very tired, and he had to let it set its own pace. If he pushed it any more, the animal would drop under him and die right there on the road. He was tired also. How long had it been since he had slept? Oh yes, ten, twelve hours earlier in the evening, before that pale boy had come with the news of Villega's capture. Mallory's body ached and his spine was sore. He had never ridden so far so fast in his life. Not even during the worst days in Ireland.

He half-dozed for a while, popping awake at every unexpected sound. He guessed that though his route was slightly longer, he'd arrive in Mesa Verde before the troops. They would stop a few times to rest, and given the hour, probably to cook a meal. He thought about Juan. Under any circumstances, by the time they got back to the city Juan would have the soldiers believing he was just a dumb, innocent pimp who'd gone to the cave because a messenger had said there were these men in the hills who wanted some women. To him, it was just a business deal. Then when he'd seen the bodies, he'd attacked the soldiers because he thought there were only two of them and that they were bandits. How could he know they were soldiers?

But there weren't other circumstances. Juan's sons were dead. He'd be breathing hatred and defiance. The soldiers would probably punch him about some during the ride in.

Mallory was passing high grass now. In a short while he'd be going through farmland. He took off his coat and draped it across the horse's neck.

Chapter Seven

Mesa Verde proved to be quiet. With word out about the night's shootings, the citizens seemed to be staying even more to their homes than during the height of the rebel fighting. And there weren't many troops about either, just an occasional soldier sleepily standing guard at key buildings. The others must be snugly in bed, Mallory thought, resting up after their night's work. Mallory rode calmly down the center of the street without being challenged.

He left his horse at a livery a few blocks from the garrison. The proprietor took him for a German and was very solicitous. Mallory told the man he was a mining engineer. Was there any place he could buy dynamite and blasting caps? He needed it back at the mine.

"No, *señor*," the man said. "The soldiers do not permit it."

Mallory walked cautiously toward the fort. He passed a saloonkeeper opening his door for the day, and the man nodded to him. The smell of frying sausages wafted out from the tavern and made his stomach stir.

He had to get some explosives. Somewhere in the city there would be some, even if under lock, key, and armed guard. He couldn't go around asking civilians where they were; that would be too suspicious. He'd have to find out at the source, from the troops themselves.

The garrison was a low stone building of two stories with a large courtyard. The yard and the building were

114

surrounded by an eight-foot stone wall. Mallory circled it from a distance, keeping out of view behind the shops and houses. There were two entrances to the garrison, one on either side of the building, each with an iron door guarded by two soldiers. He wondered if the explosives were stored within.

Mallory picked out the youngest and dumbest-looking soldier and, stepping out into the street, walked toward him. He buttoned and smoothed his coat and set his hat at a respectable angle on his head. The soldier didn't notice him until he was a few feet away.

The boy turned and brought his rifle up lazily. On the far side of the door, his burly companion came to attention.

"What are you doing here?" the young soldier asked.

Mallory flashed him a stern look. "Young man, change your tone with me."

The boy stiffened and looked confusedly at his companion. He turned back to Mallory. "Excuse me," he said uncertainly. "But I must ask all visitors their business."

"My name is Eugene Graham and I am a representative of British-Mexican Exploration, Ltd.," Mallory said. "As you probably know, we lease mining lands in the North Sierras. I came into town now to purchase explosives which are vitally necessary for our operations, only to be told that the army had confiscated all blasting material. Unless I am immediately provided with the needed materials, I shall have to telegraph President Huerta and inform him of the matter."

The boy's eyes widened. "We don't keep explosives here," he mumbled nervously. "Only ammuniton. The explosives are in a storehouse behind the tax assessor's office. You will have to see the lieutenant there."

"Which way is the office?"

The youth gave him directions.

"Thank you very much. I shall commend you to the lieutenant."

Only the lieutenant and two other men were on duty at the assessor's storehouse, a squat adobe structure with a thin metal roof. The guard there must have been stripped for the assault into the mountains, Mallory guessed. Gutierrez would have considered that a heavy guard was no longer necessary, now that he was about to round up the rebels.

Mallory strolled casually up to the lieutenant as he sat on a bench under the warehouse portico. The two guards stood inattentively at the door. They clearly expected no trouble.

The lieutenant had a doughy, characterless face. He raised it indifferently to Mallory and asked, "What do you want?" in a tone that said he didn't care to be bothered.

Mallory told him he was Eugene Graham, mining representative.

"Oh? You have any identification?" the lieutenant asked sourly.

"Yes, of course." Mallory reached inside his coat. His hand came out holding a gun. The lieutenant and the two soldiers looked at it and quickly up at his face. He smiled, and the smile froze them.

"Unlock the door," he ordered.

He herded them into the windowless building and made them lie face down on the dirt floor. The room was dim and steamy. Boxes of dynamite lined one wall. At the back barrels of powder were stacked to the ceiling. Along another wall were caps and fuses.

And something else.

Leaning against some of the cartons was a black metal machine that set Mallory's heart pounding against his ribs. Incredibly, there before him stood a motorcycle, a sleek, obviously new, very large and powerful bike. It was German made, Mallory recognized immediately. One of the finest machines he'd ever seen. "Whose is that?" he asked.

The lieutenant raised his head. "The tax assessor's."

"Thank him for me later, would you?"

Mallory loaded his coat pockets with dynamite, fuses, and caps. He pushed still more dynamite into the motor-cycle's pouches, then wheeled the machine to the door. "If the three of you take turns, you should be able to dig your way out of here in less than a day," he said. "Or if you get lucky maybe somebody'll miss you before that." He pulled the door closed and snapped the lock. The door was too heavy for them to break down, and nobody would hear them if they screamed.

Across from the garrison, Mallory remembered, was a small restaurant. A picture of it flashed to mind. It was within a stone's throw of the far end of the garrison courtyard. The building had a flat roof, didn't it? He was certain it wasn't sloped. A flat roof with an abutment, a small wall, facing the street. It would be perfect.

He stayed with the alleyways. Nobody saw him. When he reached the restaurant, Mallory parked the machine behind a small shed in the side alley, checking it first to determine whether it had gasoline. It did. If the restaurant owner didn't come out, the motorcycle would be safe there.

He went round back and discovered, to his pleasure, that the back wall was easily scaled. A moment later he was flat out on the roof, hiding behind the two-foot-high front wall, watching the garrison through a hole in the adobe.

It wasn't until an hour later that they brought Juan in. The sun had begun to burn away the clouds, and Mallory was hot and uncomfortable on the roof. His eyes burned with sweat. He saw them ride past with Juan, who stared stonily ahead.

They turned the corner and stopped at the gate. Mallory heard an order growled, and Juan dismounted. In a moment they had vanished inside.

He gave them an hour at the most. That was all it would take to satisfy themselves that Juan knew nothing. He waited 15 minutes and then slipped down from the roof. In the shed beside the building he found an old piece of canvas. It would be perfect. He wrapped the canvas around four sticks of dynamite.

Mallory walked directly away from the garrison, circled a block and came up on the same side of the street as the garrison wall. The street was clear. He strolled casually along the wall and, when he was opposite the restaurant, dropped the package. He walked another dozen feet, cut across the road and circled another block until he was back at the rear of the restaurant.

From the roof he could see his package nestled against the garrison wall. In the dirty canvas it looked like someone's garbage.

They brought Juan out twenty minutes later. The soldiers pushed him roughly toward Mallory's end of the courtyard. Mallory could see as Juan came toward him that his face was reddish and badly bruised.

The garrison wall to the left of the wall facing Mallory was painted with white stripes. You better use that goddamned wall, you bastards, Mallory thought. He held his breath as the soldiers came forward, then relaxed when they pushed Juan against the stripes, rather than against the wall with the explosives.

He blew them a little kiss, then brought out from under his coat his pistol and a stick of dynamite.

The firing squad took up position facing Juan. The Mexican glared at them icily. "Platoon!" an officer called. Mallory lit the fuse to the dynamite stick. He waited. "Ready!" the officer snapped. Mallory stood up suddenly. "Aim!" Mallory heaved the dynamite with all his strength in the direction of the firing squad.

Mallory saw Juan look up at that moment and instinctively duck. The dynamite sailed toward the soldiers. It exploded with an enormous bang, and the squad disappeared in a cloud of black smoke.

Mallory braced himself against the shock wave. The moment it passed he took aim at the canvas package and squeezed off three quick shots. The second explosion knocked him on his back.

He got up quickly and ran to the rear of the roof. His blood pounding in his ears, he dropped to the ground and raced for the motorcycle. Goddamn, it better start the first time. Every second counted.

It did. The motorcycle roared to life and settled into a sweet purr. Christ, this is a fine machine, he found himself thinking as he pushed it toward the smoking ruins of the wall.

He took the rubble full out, praying that a tire wouldn't go. The machine climbed it, paused for a frightening second, then hurtled into the air and down the other side.

The courtyard was still churning thick smoke. Shouts were coming from the garrison. In a minute the troops inside would come rushing out, shooting.

Mallory headed for where Juan had been. The machine bounced over a few bodies before he swerved sharply to the left and stopped. Juan was standing there, grinning. Mallory reached out, grabbed his collar and pulled him toward the rear seat. Juan jumped on.

Mallory spun the motorcycle and it plunged back toward the hole in the wall. With the smoke lifting, he was able to see enough to guide it through a narrow space nearly clear of debris. Behind him, Juan was screaming curses at the soldiers.

Free of the courtyard, Mallory opened the bike fully. They were a block away before the first shots rang out vainly behind them.

PART THREE

JOHNNY AND JOHNNY

Chapter One

Juan peered out through the slats of the cattle car. A peon with a sickly look was leaning against the end wall of the station platform. The peon was dead. Juan had just seen him executed by a firing squad, but the man's body stubbornly refused to fall.

Two soldiers walked wearily over and pushed the body to the ground. One of them threw a straw mat over the body and they rolled the peon in it. Finished, they dragged the man over beside a line of rolled mats. Juan counted nine rolls.

An enormous crowd was milling on the platform itself, fighting to get on the train. At the far end of the platform, soldiers and police were struggling in vain to hold back a screaming, surging mass of civilians. In the distance Juan could hear the dull thud of cannon fire.

The peasants on the platform were carrying bundles which must have contained their lives' possessions. Herds of children clawed at their parents, wailing hysterically as they were pummeled to and fro by the mob. Here and there Juan could see a bewildered soldier trying to push his way through. Policemen were clubbing the peasants back from the train with their rifle butts, men and women alike, hoping to maintain some order. The few wretched old passenger cars were already filled beyond belief.

Juan noticed two particularly determined soldiers fight through the panicky crowd and haul a civilian off the train. They dragged him through the pressing mass of flesh, holding him with one hand each while wielding their free forearms as bludgeons. They smashed their way to Juan's end of the platform, then pulled the man off it and stood him by the end wall.

A captain came over to the civilian and glowered at him. The captain reached out and, with a violent pull, tore off the man's shirt. Juan was surprised to see a lieutenant's uniform underneath.

The captain ripped off the lieutenant's insignia. His mouth curled in contempt. "The fact that President Huerta has abandoned the capital doesn't mean a thing," he growled. "And above all it doesn't authorize an officer to desert."

He turned to the soldiers. "Shoot him!"

The two soldiers slammed the disheveled lieutenant against the wall. The man's features came apart in terror. "Turn around!" the captain snapped scornfully. "Deserters are shot in the back."

A fearful moan escaped the lieutenant. Reluctantly, he turned to face the wall. A second later his body was hurled against the stone by a volley of shots; it fell in a heap to the ground.

Behind him Juan heard mingled bleating, braying, clucking, and grunting. He turned around. There were no cattle in the car, only goats and sheep and cages of chickens, rabbits, and geese. The crates were piled along one wall of the car; along the other were stacked flour sacks, oil kegs, and wine barrels. Juan had presumed at first that the supplies and animals were for troops up north, but something else made him doubt that. In the corner was an enormous cage holding a covey of variously colored and assorted birds. Only a collector would have them; they were clearly not for eating. Juan wondered who the collector might be.

In the other corner Mallory lay stretched out on a pile of straw, his bowler over his eyes. Juan regarded him with something akin to fondness. Firecracker had proved to be okay after all.

He kicked a goat out of the way and went over and cleared a place in the straw for himself. With a sigh, he stretched out beside Mallory. He noticed as he eased his sombrero over his face that there was another bird cage directly overhead.

A minute later there was a loud plop, followed by a faint dripping sound. Ugh! Juan sat up and examined his hat. The bird dropping lay directly in the middle, a slimy, malodorous stain. Juan looked wearily up at the bird cage and shook his head. "Ah, but for the rich, you sing . . ." he told the bird.

He lay back down and put the sombrero back over his face.

"We should reach the American border by tonight," Mallory said without stirring. He sounded optimistic.

Juan didn't say anything. They were going to America, sure, but the idea no longer excited him. America made him think of banks and banks made him think of his *niños*.

Mallory tried again. "Hey, what was that idea of yours. . . ? Our company, wasn't it, uh, 'Johnny and Johnny' . . ."

Juan lifted his hat and smiled sadly and thinly at Mallory. He was grateful for the Irishman's try, anyway.

"Forget it, Irish," he said softly.

He rolled back over. The straw smelled sweet. It was good to lay in it after the long ride from Mesa Verde. His backside still ached from that hard rear seat and his arms were stiff from hanging on for so long. They had made it within five miles of Orozco and then walked the rest of the way to the city. A train was preparing to leave for the north, they had learned, and so they had stolen onto the cattle car under cover of darkness. In a day, maybe two, they'd be in America and away from this insane war. Juan dozed off.

They were jolted awake by a heavy thud. There was a sound of metal clanging and the cattle car lurched violently forward, then stopped. A chicken coop fell with a clatter. The birds fluttered frantically inside it.

Mallory got up quickly and looked through the slats. Behind, two railroad workers were finishing the task of coupling another wagon to the cattle car. Armor plating had been bolted over the entire surface of the new car. Even the doors and windows were shielded, leaving only small openings for weapons. A soldier stood on each footboard.

On the platform other soldiers were now brutally beating the peons aside. They formed a semicircular clearing to the armored car and held it against the swelling, shouting throng.

A horn began to honk in short, edgy bursts. Mallory's ears picked up. Straight ahead another detachment of soldiers came marching toward the clearing. In their midst was a large, heavy sedan. The automobile was of fine polished wood set off by gleaming brass. With the windows raised and reflecting the intense sunlight, Mallory couldn't see who was riding inside.

The vehicle eased into the cleared area and the cordon of soldiers immediately began unloading suitcases and carrying them to the train. Mallory lost count after the first half dozen cases.

A chauffeur climbed out of the sedan and opened the rear door. A stocky man stepped out in a regal manner, head up, not looking at the frantic peasants. He was clutching a bulging red leather bag. The man wore a lavishly expensive dark suit, and his soft gray hair had obviously been trimmed by an expert barber. Mallory recognized him immediately.

It was the governor. The man whose face was plastered on posters all over Mesa Verde and Orozco. The grandfatherly "gentleman" who gave bread to peasants.

Mallory frowned. He glanced uneasily at Juan. If the

Mexican saw His Excellency Don Jaime now, all those soldiers wouldn't prevent him from trying to kill the man. Juan caught his glance and started to rise.

"What are they doing out there?" he asked.

Mallory wheeled around. "Nothing!" he smiled. He slapped Juan's shoulder reassuringly and gently but forcefully pushed him back down. "They just hooked up the locomotive, that's all. We'll be leaving soon. Might as well catch some sleep."

With a grunt, Juan stretched out again.

Mallory peeked through the slats. The governor was being escorted aboard the train. He held the red bag under his arm as a drowning man would a lifesaver. Dozens of soldiers boarded the armored car with him.

Mallory went over and sat down against the back wall of the cattle car, the wall separating it from the governor's coach. The smell of animal dung stung his nose. He smiled to himself. If Juan knew about the armored car, he'd say the smell from there was worse. He watched the Mexican intently, relaxing only when he appeared to be heavily asleep.

Ten minutes later the train began to move. Mallory saw the crowds and the station slip by. Within minutes, the train was moving at a smooth and steady speed. The cattle car swayed gently, lulling Mallory into a state of wakeful consciousness.

It wasn't for two hours that the guerrillas attacked.

Juan felt himself slam against a hard surface. Something heavy and pointed landed on his back and made him cry out. He looked up dazedly. The train had stopped. The animals were bleating and screaming in terror. Crazed, they jostled each other back and forth. In the spilled cages, chickens and geese fluttered madly while the rabbits ran in frenzied circles. The supply crates lay everywhere.

Outside, heavy machine guns were chattering incessantly. Juan looked at Mallory, sprawled against the back wall. They exchanged worried looks.

"Motherofjesus!" Juan leaped toward the slats. He pressed his face against them, peering toward the front of the train. He could just make out the ends of tree trunks lying across the tracks in front of the locomotive. A barricade! But why? Who? The rebels? Why attack a trainful of peons and a handful of stupid goats and shitting birds? Were those madmen really as moronic as he thought?

They were stopped on the plain. A dry, rocky terrain stretched unbroken for miles. Guerrillas could be seen shooting from behind the rocks. Judging from the angle of their fire, Juan thought, there must be targets on the roof of the train.

Dozens of guerrillas suddenly broke from behind the rocks and raced for the rear of the train. Toward the cattle car? Toward him? It couldn't be! And yet there they were, firing insanely in his direction. A few bullets ripped through the planking, showering splinters into the car. You idiots! Juan screamed to himself.

Again, he followed the angle of their fire. No, they weren't shooting at him. They were aiming past the cattle car. He looked sharply to his right. Hah! There was another car there, one covered with thick black plates. There must be troops inside it.

There was a rattling noise in the car. Juan looked toward Mallory. The handle to the end door of the cattle car was jumping up and down above Mallory's head. The Irishman glanced up quizzically. Someone was trying to escape from the armored car, Juan realized suddenly.

Mallory's face was as imperturbable as ever. He got up slowly and backed against the wall beside the door. Then he reached out and coolly opened the inside lock to the door.

The door swung open cautiously. A man stepped into the car. He was in shirtsleeves and his pants were partly unbuttoned. His left hand held tightly to a red leather bag. His right hand held a pistol.

Startled, the man jumped at the sight of Juan and brought up the gun. Juan regarded him with curiosity. Who was he? He frowned. Something about the man was familiar.

The man extended the gun at him and sighted along it. His hand was trembling. "Get out of the way," he said.

Juan didn't move. He was worried now. Why couldn't he place the man? He was sure he had seen him before. He looked at the red bag. What was in it?

The man cocked the pistol.

Mallory acted then. He came swiftly away from the wall at the man's left and chopped his hand quickly and powerfully down on the wrist holding the gun. With his other hand he caught the weapon in his bowler. Juan smiled. A nice trick!

The man shrunk upon himself visibly. He looked from Juan to Mallory in alarm and then back to Juan. His chest heaved in short, fierce gasps. Outside, the gunfire and shouting grew closer and more intense.

"What do you want from me?" the man wheezed. "Let me by. . . ."

Something about the way he held his head struck Juan. He studied the soft, quivering flesh of the man's face. And suddenly he knew.

The realization jolted him. The posters! The governor! Don Jaime himself! That pompous, thieving son of a diseased mother! Huerta's pimp. Guiterrez' master. That bread he was pictured handing out to the peasants, it was poisoned. The man was a murderer.

Don Jaime was cringing now, clearly intimidated by the silence. He glanced pathetically down at the bag he was holding, then tossed it at Juan. It fell heavily to the floor. "Open it, it's yours," he stammered. He brought his hands up imploringly. "There's a fortune inside. Money, jewels, deeds. Let me go. It's yours. You can have it all. Everything. . . ."

Juan said nothing. A raucous din, very loud now, drifted into the cattle car. It melded into a fierce howl which seemed to shake the train and which set the animals bleating again. The guerrillas were assaulting the armored car.

He glanced at Mallory and slowly held out his hand. The Irishman nodded, understanding. He reached into the bowler and tossed the pistol to Juan.

"No," Don Jaime whimpered. "No. . . ."

Juan stared at him coldly and aimed the weapon. An icy rage had gripped him. He would have his revenge. He would have the eye, tooth, and hand of this squealing pig.

Don Jaime stumbled sideways. Mad with fear, he scrambled toward the gate of the car. A sour odor came off the man. He tripped over a sack and fell forward onto the straw, but clawed his way quickly to his feet. The pistol followed him implacably.

The armored car behind them was shaking now. Loud thumping and ringing cracks issued from it. The rebels must be on it. The shooting had stopped. Gradually, the shouting was dying down.

Don Jaime staggered into a goat. A craven shriek escaped him. He clambered over the animal and lunged for the gate. His hands tore at it frantically. With a final, fearful heave he managed to slide it open a crack. Juan watched it all in silence.

Don Jaime turned for the small opening. Juan saw him outlined briefly against a pale blue sky. In a moment he would leap. Juan shot him in the shoulder.

The bullet spun him around. His face was the most frightened and pained Juan had ever seen. There was no further that terror could take a man, he suddenly understood. He shot the creature before him in the eye.

It made no further sound. Blood spurted upward from its eye as it fell backward through the gate. A second later

Juan could see only the sky's soft blue before him. He was dimly aware that the shouting had begun again almost instantly after Don Jaime had fallen out.

Something in him cracked. A strange feeling overcame him. The dull, rootless pain he had felt that night at the cave seemed to wash away. He stood still a minute, his mind casting up images at an incredible rate, taking him back and forward and back again to visions which he had thought were dead. The old, compelling excitement rushed back into him like a flood.

Mallory had moved to close the sliding doors. He glanced out through the slats as the door banged into place, then turned to Juan. "Doesn't look like this train will ever reach America," he said resignedly.

"Maybe the train won't. But we will."

Juan looked down at the governor's bag. He was beginning to feel more lightheaded and exuberant by the moment. He had just killed the governor, maybe the most corrupt man in Mexico, hadn't he? And the governor was fleeing with all his money, jewels and deeds, wasn't he? And here they were at his, Juan's, feet. Who needed banks now? Who needed anything? Here was a fortune, more money than he'd ever seen. And it was his. His.

He bent and picked up the bag. Mallory looked at him in surprise.

"Which way is America, Johnny?" Juan said.

In America he could safely spend it. In America he could live like a rich man without those insane rebels plaguing him. In America they understood his kind of man.

Mallory crossed to the opposite gate. His expression was impassive once again. "I think it's this way, straight ahead," the Irishman said.

"So what are we waiting for?" His head sang with America. He would own the finest horses and the best automobiles and the most beautiful women. Motherofjesus, he would be a king.

"You really want to go, huh?" Mallory said.

He nodded. America was the place. No more petty banditry. No more filthy whores. A rich man in America was like a rich man nowhere else; he could buy a whole state for himself. He could even . . . he could even buy his own bank.

Mallory pushed back the gate and stepped aside.

"Let's go," Juan bellowed, and rushed blindly for the door. Delirious with his fantasies, his body burning in feverish anticipation, he hurled himself into space.

And landed amidst a throng of exultant guerrillas.

Chapter Two

Cheering madly, the guerrillas lifted Juan in the air and settled him atop their shoulders. Their swollen, triumphant cries rang in the air. Dazed, Juan looked desperately back at Mallory. Mallory smiled. It was Mesa Verde all over again, he thought. Hail the conquering hero, that poor bastard! When they wrote the history of the revolution there would be a paragraph about Juan. The man who freed the Mesa Verde prisoners. The man who had killed the despised Don Jaime. What had Wilde said about heroes? That they represented a failure of the imagination by the unimaginative.

Mallory got down slowly from the cattle car. Instantly, he was surrounded by excited, backslapping guerrillas who looked at him as if he were some demigod. The friend of the great man is automatically a great man himself, he mused.

Juan was still looking at him imploringly. He clutched the red bag under his arm and twisted frantically around in the supporting arms to watch Mallory as the rebels bore him to the front of the train. Mallory smiled thinly up at him and looked away. To his right, a group of guerrillas was dragging Don Jaime's body by the feet. The running wound where his eye had been glared obscenely into the sun.

Still jabbering and pounding him, the guerrillas steered Mallory along behind Juan. From the front of the train another large group of rebels approached them. Leading them was a giant of a man, one of the biggest men Mallory had ever seen. He had a thick moustache and wore his hair long for a Mexican, almost to his neck. Ammunition belts crisscrossed his massive chest. He was beaming up at Juan as he came forward.

Mallory saw the guerrillas suddenly grasp Juan and hurl him with a shout at the big man. The man caught him against his chest as he might a doll and hugged him in a warm, fraternal embrace. Then he set Juan down before him, stepped back and opened his arms.

"Juan Miranda!" he roared. "The hero of Mesa Verde!!"

"Huh, who told you that?"

The man pointed to two guerrillas. "They did. They were there. You freed them. They recognized you immediately." He clapped Juan on the shoulder, and the Mexican's burly frame shook under the blow. "And they tell me you killed that animal, Don Jaime, and threw him out to them. Hah! You'll be more famous than Villa soon." His eyes dropped to the red bag. He reached out and plucked it easily from Juan's grasp. "Ay, and what's this?"

The big man opened the bag. He whistled. "Incredible! What a fortune!"

Mallory had moved just to the side of Juan. He saw the Mexican's face pale into bewilderment, then turn hard— as hard as he'd ever seen it. The pistol was in Juan's belt, Mallory noticed. He watched Juan's hand.

"And who the hell are you?" Juan breathed. He glared balefully at the big man.

The man handed the red bag to a small, wiry guerrilla beside him. "Florestano Santerna," he announced grandly. "Commander of Villa's advanced forces." He put an arm around Juan's shoulder and turned him back toward the cattle car. "The general's heard about you. He wants to meet you."

Juan looked dumbstruck. "Me?"

"Sure. He knows what you've done. The head of the revolutionary committee told us everything——"

Mallory heard another voice, a too familiar one, break in. "Never enough . . ." the voice said.

Mallory saw Juan turn in surprise to his left. He followed the Mexican's gaze. Villega stood among the rebels, his thin body seeming thinner than ever, almost lost in the crowd.

Villega's face was heavily scarred. Mallory stared at him. An icy hand gripped his spine. How had Villega explained Mesa Verde? How had he explained those scars? Couldn't these bastards put two and two together?

"Hey, Doc!" Juan gushed in genuine surprise. Mallory saw him surge toward Villega and grasp his arms. "This is really——" Juan turned to his right. His eyes searched out Mallory. "Hey, Irish, look who's here."

Villega looked toward him with a smile. Something in Mallory's expression visibly startled him. Villega's face went ashen. Mallory found himself thinking about guilt complexes as he made his way through the crowd. His eyes never left Villega.

He stopped before the doctor and stared at him. Villega smiled wanly. "John!" he said. "Nice to see you." His voice was weak.

He extended his hand. Mallory noticed that it was trembling slightly. Villega must be wondering whether he, Mallory, could possibly know. "Me too," Mallory said blandly. He reached out and gave Villega a quick handshake. The doctor's hand felt frail and cold.

Santerna was signaling for attention. He raised his treetrunk arms and waved them until the rebels fell silent. Then he shouted, "Everybody on the train. We'll drop the passengers at the next station and then we're going to meet Pancho Villa. We're going to the revolution! The REVOLUTION!!!!"

Whooping frenziedly, the mass of guerrillas broke for the train, pushing past Mallory and Juan. The rebels stormed onto the already overloaded cars and clambered onto the roof. They filled the locomotive, the cattle car, and the armored car to capacity.

Juan grabbed Mallory's arm and pulled him toward the open plain. A flying grasshopper fluttered up and buzzed away from them.

"Hey, what are you doing?" Mallory said. He knew before Juan answered.

"What do you mean, what am I doing? Gutierrez wants me. Villa wants me. You have to ask what I'm gonna do?"

Mallory pulled away. Juan needed some more Irish practicality and a little less Latin blood. "We're going to get on that train because if you try to get away now those men will tear you to pieces."

"But Jesus Christ, I'm their hero!"

Mallory threw him a strained look. "Heroes don't run in that direction when the revolution is in the other direction." He nodded toward the head of the train. "Only cowards do."

Juan's lips twisted into bitterness. He started to speak, changed his mind and stalked off toward the train, pushing his way through a few laggard guerrillas. Mallory followed him.

The train was hot and noisy. The rebels buzzed incessantly, talking of battles never fought but already won. Outside, a gray dusk was filtering down like dust settling on a mirror.

They had been traveling for two hours and the passengers had long since been let off. The train was filthy and the seats were splitting. Flies swam through it in thick clusters.

Mallory sat in a corner seat in the crowded car. The smell of sweat and of cheap, acrid tobacco hung in the air. He would have liked a cool bath just then. He would have liked a warm woman better, he thought.

Santerna slept on the seat beside him. His huge body crowded Mallory into the window. Across from Santerna Juan was also sleeping. Both men had their heads back against the seat and were snoring.

Villega was seated directly opposite Mallory. The doctor had sat there quietly, visibly uneasy, since they'd boarded the train. Now with Juan and Santerna asleep he was trying to make conversation. Mallory stared at him in silence, not moving, absorbed in thought.

"Latest news says that Villa has reached the outskirts of Mexico City," Villega began tentatively. He studied Mallory for reaction. Mallory showed none. "A few weeks ago it was only a dream—"

He broke off, clearly embarrassed by Mallory's unfaltering gaze, and looked out the window. How the hell had he gotten away with it, Mallory wondered again? Somebody must have suspected. A hundred rebels don't get slaughtered without someone asking questions. Not when their leader shows up alive and with torture marks. What kind of story could Villega have told them?

The doctor turned back to him. "Let's hope for all of us the future—" Mallory's stare forced him again to look away in embarrassment. He finished the sentence gazing at the fleeting countryside. "—is able to erase all the ugliness and sadness of the past."

He fell silent. A fly landed on his hand and he flicked it away. Mallory only barely saw the movement. What was it Villega said? Erase the past . . . ? The gentle bumping of the train lulled him. The ugliness and sadness. . . ? Mallory's eyes glazed over. Villega's face became watery and distant.

He saw himself in that pub in Ireland. He saw the tortured, surprised face of Nolan, the eyes crying for help, before Nolan grasped at his stomach and crumbled to the floor. Those pitiful eyes begged him for something until the very last moment. Begged him for what . . . for understanding? For forgiveness?

He saw himself back slowly out of the pub. And he saw . . . no, he heard the deep, mournful horn of a departing ship. He was on the ship. He was on it looking back at the coast of Ireland in the morning mist. It was green and brown and there was a small gray house of stone at the end of the quay. The horn blew sadly on, and the mist closed round the quay until it was just a memory.

His eyes cleared and he found himself looking at the back of a newspaper. Villega was reading. Probably so as not to have to look at me, Mallory thought.

He gazed absently at the back of the paper until the screeching of brakes jolted him alert. The train lurched violently and slammed to a halt. Juan was thrown almost into Santerna's lap.

"Hey, what the—"

Santerna shook himself awake. All around the car men were scrambling to their feet and pushing their heads out the windows. "What the hell is it?" Santerna roared.

A peon brought his chalky face back in. "There's a barricade across the tracks. It looks like some of our *compadres* up there."

A moment later the door burst open and a bearded young rebel climbed in. "Who's Santerna?" he said excitedly.

"I am."

"We've got a message for you. An army train has left Parral and is heading toward you."

"What about Villa?"

"He met resistance on the Sierra. He's sent word that you must hold out for at least twenty-four hours once the soldiers attack you. Gutierrez knows you're coming and is planning to cut you off."

Mallory watched Santerna. His lips had gone bloodless and were now edged in a taut line. He looked puzzled and betrayed. He turned to Villega.

"You said a train," the doctor said to the young guerrilla. "How many soldiers?"

"More than a thousand. With cavalry and heavy weapons."

An anxious rumble swept through the train. "Quiet!" Santerna barked. He was sweating heavily. He pulled a grimy old piece of paper from his pocket and unfolded it across his lap. A map.

Mallory leaned around the huge man's shoulder and planted his finger on the map. "We're here, right?" he said calmly. Santerna eyed him curiously. Mallory studied the map a moment. "Huh, not even a canyon or a bridge." He tapped the paper. "There's only this hill. How long do we have before we get there?"

"Two hours, more or less."

"Will we get there before Gutierrez?"

"Yes."

"Well, then, it seems to me we'll have to stop them here."

Santerna shook his head impatiently. "All it takes is unbolting two yards of track. But what then? They'll still slaughter us."

"There's more than one way to stop a train."

Juan broke in suddenly. "You got any dynamite?"

"We've got about one hundred pounds," Santerna said.

Juan turned to Mallory. "That enough for you?" He sounded thoroughly businesslike. Mallory wondered what the hell he was planning now. He dismissed the notion. Why worry about it?

"It'll have to be. I'll need the locomotive as well. And I don't think you'll get it back." He pushed his bowler to the back of his head, leaned back and thought a moment.

"I'll also need one other man," he said nonchalantly. "Somebody with courage, faithful to the cause." He didn't want to lay it on too thick.

Juan took the bait. He sighed heavily and said, with resignation, "All right. All right. What do you want me to do?" Ah, so the slippery son-of-a-bitch was scheming to get away on the locomotive.

Mallory ignored him. "Somebody like Doctor Villega," he said, turning toward the man. His eyes burned into him.

Villega stiffened and an almost imperceptible shadow of fear flickered across his face. He forced a smile. A fly buzzed between Mallory and the doctor and flew off.

"It will be an honor," Villega said huskily.

Chapter Three

The headlights of the locomotive cut through the night. They illuminated gleaming track rushing away from the backing locomotive and low brown scrub along the ground. The night was pale and warm, with a half moon casting dim gray light through a thin cloud cover.

Mallory checked the pressure gauge. It was too low. He looked at Villega, his scarred face pink and sweating in the red glow from the open boiler. Villega was in shirtsleeves. His thin frame bent and threw shovel after shovel of coal into the boiler.

"Step on it, Villega," Mallory snapped. "I need more pressure in this baby."

The doctor obeyed automatically. He doubled his effort. His heavy breathing could be heard above the clatter of the engine.

Mallory took off his bowler and wiped his forehead. He replaced the hat and looked out the window, watching the engine back into the night. He guessed they had almost gone far enough. A mile would do it nicely. He glanced toward the front of the engine and beyond the headlight, trying to make out the shadow of the hill where the guerrillas lay hidden. He couldn't see anything from that distance.

He stopped the engine and shut down the headlight. Darkness swallowed them. He let the engine sit, his eye on the pressure gauge, the boiler hissing softly. How long had it been since he'd run a train? Was it ten years, fifteen

years since he'd been a good laboring man? And then it
had only been for six months.

He turned to Villega. The doctor set the shovel down
and inhaled deeply. He looked at Mallory. He seemed to
be steeling himself to say something. Mallory waited.

Villega inhaled again. "Let's stop playacting, Mallory,"
he said softly. "You know everything, don't you? You
either sensed it . . . or guessed it."

"It's much simpler than that. I saw you, Villega. That
night . . . in the lorry."

"I see."

Villega grimaced. His eyes closed momentarily. "And
you've already judged and condemned me?"

Mallory moved toward the shovel. "You killed the
children of a friend of mine, you know?"

"Juan?"

"Yeah."

Villega fell silent. Mallory picked up the shovel and
hurled a heavy load of coal into the boiler.

"How'd you fool them, Villega?" he grunted, shoveling
in more coal. "How'd you get them to take you back with
all that artwork on your face?"

"I told them it wasn't I who had informed. That it was
one of the men who was shot. I told them I was arrested
with the others and saved for torture because of my
position with the revolutionary committee."

"And they believed you?"

"I had a witness."

Mallory looked up in surprise. "Who?"

"A boy. A soldier whose father had been killed by
Huerta and who wanted to join the cause. He was the one
who helped me escape."

"And he lied for you?"

"He knew what they had done to me. He understood
what it had been like."

"Where is he now?"

"He's dead. He was killed in some fighting in Orozco."

"How convenient."

Villega looked pained.

Mallory asked: "How did Gutierrez know Santerna was on his way to help Villa?"

"It wasn't from me."

Mallory studied his face.

"You *have* judged and condemned me," Villega said. "That's why you brought me with you, isn't it? To kill me!"

Mallory didn't answer. He turned back to the coal and shoveled in silence.

Villega seemed to give off as much tension as the boiler did heat. He stood faintly quivering for a moment, unnerved by Mallory's silence, then exploded in exasperation: "Oh, sure, it's easy to judge! But have you ever been tortured? Are you sure . . . sure you wouldn't talk? I was sure. And instead . . . I talked. And now am I supposed to kill myself? Why? For what? The dead stay dead. But me, I haven't changed. I still believe in the same things. I can still be useful to the cau——"

Mallory felt his blood suddenly rage through him. He dropped the shovel and grabbed for Villega's collar, twisting until he bent Villega's leathery neck, strangling him. "Shut up, Villega. For God's sakes, shut up!"

He let go his own breath and then released Villega's collar. He sighed and looked away, staring absently at the glistening pressure gauge. "I don't judge you," he said softly, almost to himself. "I only did that once in my life."

He felt drained. "I started using dynamite because I also believed in a cause," he said. "And then I ended up believing only in dynamite." He picked up the shovel and threw it to Villega. "I don't want to kill you, Villega. I'm going to give you a chance."

Mallory looked over to the window. "Get moving with that shovel. The pressure's still too bloody low." Villega eyed him uncertainly and then returned to the task.

Mallory put his head out the window and stared into

the night ahead. It couldn't be long now. Maybe an hour at most. Maybe a good deal less. His hand tightened on the gear lever. The whole thing would be in the timing. If he got the timing right, there'd be no problem at all.

He waited. His ears adjusted to the hissing of the engine until he could pick up the sound of baying out on the plain and the whistle of the wind through the scrub. Would he hear it or see it first, he wondered? His eyes burned as they peered into the darkness.

Watching nothingness, his mind roamed back over the past year. Here he was an expatriate Irish revolutionary, a wanted man back home, sitting out on the black and sprawling Mexican Plain in a locomotive that belonged to a foreign government, ready to commit another act of war against that government. And for what? Juan was right. What was different here from anywhere else? There was always betrayal and stupidity, and things never changed for all the change. There would always be people in power and people out, corruption and revolution. There would always be loyalists and rebels, and like Juan's mice and cats they would all play out their assigned parts. And what was his part? To be a dynamiter. To hate the government and sympathize with the peasants and play that same role no matter where he was or who the opponents were. What was he doing here? He was being Mallory, the terrorist. It was all he knew. It was assigned to him. Circumstances had assigned him his personality and now that personality would dictate his fate. It was true for everyone. Personality determinism he would have called it, if he'd held a philosophy chair at Oxford.

He saw it before he heard it. A faint shower of sparks against the sky. And then, like a small lantern, the headlight glowing and round in the distance.

He watched it come on, waiting. The headlight grew larger and the shower of sparks more intense. Closer. Closer.

Now! Now! He threw the handle. It clanged in the

cabin and the engine slowly began to move. "Shovel; Villega!" Mallory shouted. "Shovel!"

The engine gathered speed. It surged forward with a dull, hollow roar from its chimney and clattered over the darkened tracks.

Mallory watched the two trains converge. Gutierrez' engineer hadn't seen them yet; there was no squeal of brakes. Good. Let them come on a little farther. Mallory watched the distance between them melt away. His lips moved silently, counting seconds, measuring space. In a moment now he could—

He came quickly back into the cab and knelt down on the floor. He already held a match in his hand. He struck it against the metal and swiftly lighted four fuses. They flared up and the dazzling sparks began worming out from the cabin, two via the window, two through the door.

Mallory stood up. Villega was staring in hypnotic fascination at the burning fuses. His eyes followed them as they disappeared outside the cabin. His face was covered with perspiration, his shirt stained with it. From the look in his eyes it could have been from fear as well as exertion.

Mallory stepped down onto the running board. The wind rushed by his head and pushed coolly against his face. The two trains were less than a half mile apart now. The other engineer would have to spot them soon. If he did, everything would be fine. They would be in perfect positions.

He glanced back at Villega. "When I say 'jump,' jump out and run. Remember, you'll be running for your life!"

Villega looked out past him at the shadowy ground rushing past. He seemed to cringe, and his breath came out in a wracking note of despair. He said nothing.

Mallory heard the first shriek of metal against metal then. His eyes followed the sparks suddenly shooting along the track ahead. The other train was braking. Christ, it would be stopping just where he wanted it. He looked toward the fuses. The sparks were halfway to the dynamite. The trains plunged toward each other. The other engineer must be frantic, Mallory thought.

They were only a quarter-mile away now. The clatter and hiss of the engine couldn't drown out the desperate whistling of the train ahead. Its headlight filled the night. Let them whistle, Mallory thought.

He reached into the cab and pulled Villega harshly toward him. "Now close your eyes and jump. Quick!"

Villega seemed frozen by fear. "No—no—! His eyes were locked in terror on the ground below. His hand was clenched in paralysis on the door grip.

Mallory looked up at the light ahead. No more time now. They were too close. He glanced at the cowering Villega. No more time for him. His breath caught and he flung himself from the engine.

He heard Villega's awful wail even before he hit. "MALLORYYYYYYYY." It pierced through all the other sounds and lingered in the air like the bottomless, unstrung cry of a dying animal. Mallory's running feet slammed into the ground and he hurtled forward. He twisted violently in mid-air, catching the second impact on his shoulder rather than his face. Pain surged through him. He relaxed and let his momentum carry him in a roll down the slope. Small rocks stabbed at him; the flesh of one hand scraped away. His breath was coming in short, wrenching gasps by the time he stopped rolling.

He looked up from the bottom of the slope, raising only his head. The locomotives were only a few hundred feet apart now. In a second they would hit. Framed against the pale red glow from the boiler was the pathetic form of Villega, still clutching desperately the doorframe grips. Villega was looking back toward where Mallory had first landed, searching for help that wasn't there.

A moment later the two engines hit. The explosion was as massive and as memorable as Mallory had ever seen.

Chapter Four

The engines crunched together and climbed skyward in a tortured ballet. They disappeared in the howling flames and smoke of the explosion.

Shards of metal flew over Mallory's head. He burrowed into the ground and brought his arms up protectively. When he looked up again, the first four or five cars of the train were lying on their sides, burning violently. Ahead of them, the engines were still cloaked in smoke; behind, most of the other cars lay twisted and smashed.

The guerrillas opened fire from the hill looming above Mallory and from the plain to the other side of the troop train. The pink glow from the fires illuminated their targets better than any flare might have done. With machine guns and rifles, they lay down a relentless barrage.

Mallory saw troops scrambling from the train and heard men screaming frantically. How many were there supposed to be? A thousand? Half of them must be dead, he guessed. That still left more troops than guerrillas. He wondered how many of their heavy weapons had been destroyed.

The soldiers were quickly organizing their defense. They were well drilled, Mallory noticed. In minutes they had several machine guns returning fire. From out of the wreckage they hauled a half-dozen mortars. They spotted them along the length of the train and began lobbing shells into the hill. The shells exploded with dull thuds.

Other troops were beginning to fire mausers at the hill.

They had positioned themselves in the wreckage so that they were protected from the merciless fire coming off the hill in front of them and from the plain behind. Mallory glanced up the hill. Among the dizzying constellation of gun flashes the troops would find plenty of targets.

A small cannon had been spilled from an open car and lay on its side beside the train. A dozen soldiers, braving the gunfire, heaved the gun upright. They lowered the barrel to zero degrees and began slinging cannister shell out into the dark countryside. Dammit, Mallory thought, they'd have to get that gun soon or it would chew up a lot of men.

In the glow from the fires he saw a slim, erect figure haul himself from one of the ruined cars. He reached the ground and, with difficulty, picked his way through the rubble. Clearly enraged, he hurled aside twisted bits of metal and dead bodies which blocked his path. Mallory saw that it was Gutierrez.

Gun in hand, the colonel made his way along the line of overturned cars, shouting orders as he went. He reached a wagon which somehow had remained upright and swung himself up through the smashed door. He looked back for moment at the hill, his face raw with hatred, before he disappeared inside.

Mallory got up and ran low toward the hill. The heated air from the fires came up and buffeted his face. The sharp, familiar cacaphony of a battle at its hilt battered his ears. He felt sore and weary in ways he never had before.

The hill wasn't too high. Running hunched over, he made it to the crest within a minute. He passed the bodies of several guerrillas along the way.

A mortar shell burst just yards in front of him and the impact threw him to the ground. He darted up quickly again and pushed ahead. All over the hill there was shouting now and men crying out in pain. If it got any worse for the rebels, he would have to do what Santerna had forbidden.

Ahead of him, in the faint light reaching the hilltop, he could make out the unmistakable figure of Juan. The Mexican was at a machine gun, swinging it determinedly back and forth along the line of the train below. Mallory headed toward him.

Juan suddenly got up and shouted indistinguishable orders to some man below him. Then he hefted the machine gun and carried it away from Mallory, toward the far end of the train. Mallory trailed him halfway down the side of the hill. He could hear someone moaning nearby and smell the sharp sting of cordite in the air.

Juan stopped to reposition the gun. He was now above the untipped car, the one into which Gutierrez had disappeared. Mallory noted the area where the gun was placed. It was right where he, Mallory, had to be if he were to finish the job properly. Juan couldn't have picked a better spot if he'd been reading his mind.

Mallory's feet slipped and sent some pebbles rolling down the hill. They struck Juan. He wheeled around, bringing the machine gun around with him. Mallory kept coming.

Juan realized who it was in time. Holding the gun, he got up and climbed toward him. He was smiling more broadly and with more genuine friendship than Mallory had thought him capable.

"Hey, Firecracker," Juan called warmly. "It's me."

The bullets caught Mallory in the side then and flung him back against the hill.

Juan was about to shoot when he recognized Mallory's silhouette coming down toward him. Motherofjesus, the Irishman was unharmed after all! And he had been worrying that somehow Mallory might not have jumped from the train in time. His own sense of relief surprised him. He was really getting to like Firecracker, he thought as he called out to him. They really were a good team. He saw Mallory smile back at him as he came down the hill.

A moment later the Irishman's body was wrenched violently around and hurled to the ground. The sight sent pain shooting into Juan's head. His heart slammed against his chest. Blood raced hotly to his eyes. With an insane scream, he turned and ran wildly down the hill. He saw Gutierrez standing in the door of the railroad car holding a rifle. The machine gun exploded in Juan's hands.

The bullets caught Gutierrez in the chest and flung him sideways against the doorframe. He bounced off into the gunfire. His body twitched and jumped like a deranged marionette, his arms flying askew. The body didn't fall until Juan's gun was empty.

Juan threw the gun down and ran frantically back up to Mallory. The Irishman lay gasping where he had fallen, his face contorted in pain. He opened his eyes as Juan neared. A taut smile edged his lips.

Juan bent to him. Mallory raised his arm and gestured weakly toward a hollow near the far edge of the hill. "Over there," he said hoarsely. "Pull me over there."

Juan grabbed him under the arms and dragged him the dozen feet to the hollow. Mallory would be safe there, at any rate. He cleared the stones and pebbles away and propped him against a rock. The Irishman's eyes remained shut all the while.

"Where the hell he get you?" Juan asked. He looked anxiously down Mallory's body.

Mallory didn't answer. Juan moved to examine the rib cage on the far side. Mallory nodded; that was the spot.

The Irishman took a rasping breath. "Right where it'll do me the most good," he said. His voice was as even and as unexcited as ever.

Juan shrugged. "Yeah, but that don't mean nothing," he lied. "You've seen worse."

"Don't be an ass."

He studied Mallory, lying there so calmly. A burning pain suddenly rose in his chest and coursed through him.

His eyes filled. He couldn't believe it, but for some reason he didn't want Mallory to die. He had never felt that way so intensely before, caring whether somebody died. But Mallory . . . Mallory was his—

He hauled in a breath. A mortar shell burst violently nearby. He never looked up. Shells were exploding all over the hill now. He didn't care.

"Jesus Christ, Johnny, and with America only two steps away!" he said, not knowing what else to say, knowing it didn't mean anything now.

Juan shook his head, disbelieving. "Listen, Firecracker . . . I mean . . . I've gotten used to you." What was he trying to say? It was all so confusing to sort out. He reached out and awkwardly gripped Mallory's arm. "Hell, you're like a . . . a brother to me. If you quit on me now, where the fuck do I go?"

Mallory smiled wearily. "Yeah, looks like I gave you a royal screw," he chided. "You'll never get those American banks now."

Juan started to reply. That wasn't what he'd meant at all. Not at all. He stopped himself. He saw that Mallory understood.

Mallory painfully sucked in air. "Stick with these lunatics," he said. "Who knows? Maybe you'll find a good deal."

A thought gnawed at Juan. Something he had to know. "What happened to Villega?" he asked.

"He's dead."

"But——"

". . . and he'll be remembered as a hero of the revolution."

"So will you!"

Mallory wheezed. His voice came out soft and remote. "Me? I'm a second-hand hero, just one of the mice." He smiled wanly. "You people can't even pronounce my name right."

Juan could see Mallory visibly fading. The lines in his face had smoothed and his mouth hung open limply. He wanted to scream at him, to call him back, but what good would it have done?

A machine gun raked the ground a few feet away. The shells pounded closer. Men were screaming below. Mallory seemed to perk up at the sound. With sudden engery, he reached into his pocket and pulled out a cigar. "Give me a light," he said.

Juan did. The crazy son-of-a-bitch could smoke a cigar if he wanted. Why the hell not? He smiled at Mallory. The pain, his, Juan's pain, didn't go away.

Mallory dragged once at the cigar. "How they doing out there?" he murmured.

"Not too good."

Mallory looked at the glowing tip of his cigar. He flashed Juan a curious smile and nodded toward his coat. Juan's eyes tracked downward. Mallory's coat lay half open. In the inside pockets, Juan saw now, were two remaining sticks of dynamite.

He stared at Mallory. The Irishman cocked his brows. His breathing was fainter but less rasping. "Come on," Mallory said, and gestured to the dynamite.

Why not? Juan took the sticks from the coat and held them out. Mallory touched the cigar to the fuses, and Juan stepped out of the hollow. He moved partway down the hill, picked out a target and hurled the first stick. He threw the second while the first was still in the air.

He cut quickly back toward the hollow. He heard the explosions behind him at the same moment he saw Mallory. The Irishman jarred him more.

Mallory had moved across the hollow. He had propped himself sideways against another rock and his eyes were following a sparkling fire that raced out the hollow and down the hill.

"No, Johnnyyy!" Juan screamed, but it was far too late.

He understood immediately. Mallory had ignored Santerna's order. Mallory had wanted to plant dynamite all along the bottom of the hill and under the track. Santerna had said no. They didn't want to destroy the entire train, just the first few cars, he had said. Just enough so that they could surprise and overwhelm the soldiers. That way they could capture the heavy weapons. They needed them badly for the assault on Mexico City. Besides, Santerna had said, there was no way they could be certain the trains would meet at the bottom of the hill.

Mallory had said he would guarantee it. The trains would meet where the dynamite lay. And the dynamite would be their insurance, in the event the battle went badly. Santerna's answer was they didn't need insurance. It hadn't been a good enough answer for Mallory, that was apparent now. He must have planted the dynamite before the rest of them arrived, while they were still marching up from the abandoned cars three miles back.

Juan rushed toward Mallory and froze. A horrible spasm shook the Irishman. His body convulsed in palsied fervor and then went limp. Mallory lay on his side, his bowler on the ground, his long hair brushing the dirt. He raised his head and grimaced, and then his eyes cleared and a light came into them for a moment and while it burned there he managed to gasp, "Duck, you sucker!" and smile for the last time.

"JOOHHHHNNNYYYYYY!!!!!"

The cry boiled despairingly out of him and hung heavily in the air as he flung himself toward his friend. The exlosion caught him and smashed him to the ground. Heat and sound and light beyond his imagination battered at his body. Flares burned in his head.

A consuming pain drove his feet madly along the ground and he thrashed toward Mallory. He caught Mallory up in his arms even as the shouting began so clamorously behind him and he stared through a veil down into the lifeless face. The pain, that awful, searing pain, stabbed at him again and he looked up blindly into the darkness ahead.

"Oh, Johnny. What about me?" he said.

The Man With No Name

in

Tandem's 'Dollar' Western Series

A Fistful of Dollars   Frank Chandler   25p

When The Man With No Name rode into town he found a chance to make a few easy dollars. But when he came to within an inch of losing his own life, he ceased to be merely dangerous – he became lethal.

The Good,
The Bad and The Ugly   Joe Millard   25p

The danger was great. The reward was the gold that two armies and a legion of dead men had failed to reclaim. To The Man With No Name the odds seemed almost favourable.

A Dollar To Die For   Brian Fox   25p

The Man With No Name found his bounty-hungry guns pitted against the greed of three desperate professional killers with a price on their heads – only one of the four could survive.

For A Few Dollars More   Joe Millard   25p

There were two of them after the same outlaw – a Mexican bandit worth $10,000 dead or alive. So they formed a partnership. It was going to be simple . . . *if* The Man With No Name didn't double-deal them all.

A Coffin Full of Dollars   Joe Millard   25p

They were a legendary threesome, out for each other's blood. Shadrach – the killer with the Y-shaped scar under his eye. Apachito – snakelike and deadly, who relished the slow death of his enemies. And The Man With No Name – hard, lean and fearless. The winner would be richer by a coffin full of dollars.

Watch out for more 'Dollar' Westerns

Westerns in Tandem editions

Occult and the Supernatural in Tandem editions

Demon Lovers   ed. Lucy Berman 25p

Witchcraft in the World Today   C. H. Wallace 25p

The Witchfinders   Ralph Comer 25p

The Mirror of Dionysos   Ralph Comer 25p

Satanism and Witchcraft   Jules Michelet 30p

Reincarnation   H. S. Santesson 25p

The Burning Court   John Dickson Carr 25p

The Vampire   Ornella Volta 25p

Witches and their Craft   Ronald Seth 30p

Real Ghosts, Restless Spirits and Haunted Minds   Brad
Steiger 25p

The Accursed   Claude Seignolle 25p

The Witches   Francoise Mallet-Joris 40p

Witchcraft For All   Louise Huebner 25p

The Open Grave   Alan Hull Walton 30p

Horror in Tandem editions

Dark Menace   Charles Birkin 17½p

So Pale, So Cold, So Fair   Charles Birkin 25p

The Unbidden   R. Chetwynd-Hayes 25p

The House of the Hatchet   Robert Bloch 25p

Play Misty For Me   Paul J. Gillette 25p

Nick Carter: the world's biggest selling spy series

Science Fiction in Tandem editions

Shield Poul Anderson 20p
The device gave total immunity to weapons – but
who would gain possession of it?

Planet of No Return Poul Anderson 25p
Man must search for colonies beyond the stars, but
can he find a permanent home there?

The Time-Hoppers Robert Silverberg 25p
Every human need was fulfilled in the 25th century,
yet they still yearned to escape

Hawksbill Station Robert Silverberg 25p
Banished from the complicated world of the far
future to the barren emptiness of the remote past

The Man in the Maze Robert Silverberg 25p
Solitary and embittered, hiding from the loathing of
his fellows, he must be lured out of his refuge to save
the world

Light a Last Candle Vincent King 25p
'Vivid stuff, a tale of internecine strife between
mutated and modified people in the far future.'
Edmund Cooper, Sunday Times

Farewell, Earth's Bliss D. G. Compton 25p
Their past was Earth, their present a colony on Mars
– and their future?

The Time Mercenaries Philip E. High 25p
They were a thousand years out of date, and the
planet's only chance to defeat the alien invaders

Donovan's Brain Curt Siodmak 25p
Doomed by disease, mangled in a plane crash, there
was no doubt that Donovan was dead. Yet his
brain lived!

Vornan 19 Robert Silverberg 30p
He appeared suddenly and mysteriously, claiming
to be a visitor from the year 2999. But his evidence
was not totally convincing.

Let The Spacemen Beware Poul Anderson 25p
Why did the gentle people of Gwydonia become like
savages at Bale-time? And was their strange be-
haviour connected with the red flower that bloomed
everywhere on the planet?

Name..

Address...

Titles required ....

....

....

....

....

....

....

....

The publishers hope that you enjoyed this book and invite you to write for the full list of Tandem titles which is available free of charge.

If you find any difficulty in obtaining these books from your usual retailer we shall be pleased to supply the titles of your choice — packing and postage 5p—upon receipt of your remittance.

WRITE NOW TO:
      Universal-Tandem Publishing Co. Ltd.,
      14 Gloucester Road,
      London SW7 4RD